BOOK TWE[LVE]

THE CURSE OF THE QUETZALCOATL

Irma Collins' concern over her father's daring archaeological
expedition to Mexico does not lessen when they return home
to Collinwood. One frightening incident after another occurs
concerning the gruesome assortment of snakes, crocodiles, and birds
Professor Collins brought back with them.

Finally, Irma has no choice but to ask her cousin Barnabas for help.

Yet there is little either can do to alter Professor Collins' devotion to
these weird animals. He refuses to part with them, and nothing —
not even the murder of innocent townspeople — will make him.

Is this how the curse of the Quetzalcoatl that was put upon her father
for disturbing the tomb of a long-dead ruler is working itself out?
Is Irma fighting just her obsessed father — or a strong supernatural
power?

Hermes Press

Published by Hermes Press, an imprint of
Herman and Geer Communications, Inc.

Daniel Herman, Publisher
Troy Musguire, Production Manager
Eileen Sabrina Herman, Managing Editor
Alissa Fisher, Graphic Design
Kandice Hartner, Senior Editor

2100 Wilmington Road
Neshannock, Pennsylvania 16105
(724) 652-0511
www.HermesPress.com; info@hermespress.com

Book design by Eileen Sabrina Herman
First printing, 2021

LCCN applied for: 10 9 8 7 6 5 4 3 2 1 0
ISBN 978-1-61345-244-8
OCR and text editing by H + G Media and Eileen Sabrina Herman
Proof reading by Eileen Sabrina Herman and Feytaline McKinley

From Dan, Sabrina, and Jacob in memory of Al DeVivo

*Acknowledgments: This book would not be possible without the help and
encouragement of Jim Pierson and Curtis Holdings*

Printed in Canada

Barnabas, Quentin and the Serpent
by Marilyn Ross

CONTENTS

CHAPTER 1

It was in 1870 that the curse of Quetzalcoatl, the feathered serpent, shadowed the estate of Collinwood. The Civil War had been over for a few years and the town of Collinsport had returned to its normal business of shipbuilding, lumbering and fishing. The spring of this particular year had been a cold, wet one for this northeast section of the Maine coast. There had even been a light snowfall in early May, but late in June the weather changed for the better and a long warm summer set in—a summer that was not to be forgotten by the residents of the isolated coastal town nor by those living at Collinwood for a long, long time.

The great, dark, sprawling mansion which dominated a high point of the cliffs overlooking the Bay of Collinsport had been deserted for a brief period following the death of its owner. The property had been willed to a cousin of the late owner, a Professor Gerald Collins, who was in Mexico on an archaeological expedition at the time of the squire's death. Word had been dispatched to the absent heir but it was not until January of 1870 that a reply came. Professor Gerald Collins wrote that he would soon be leaving Mexico and returning to the United States by means of a chartered schooner. He expected to arrive in Collinsport by late June to take up residence in the forty-room family mansion.

The news spread through the relatively small village. The family lawyer, Saul Hampstead, hired a new household and outside staff to prepare the closed mansion and its grounds for its new owner. He did this grudgingly because it had been his hope that Professor Collins would prefer not to live in the big house and would turn the property over to him to be sold. The crafty, middle-aged lawyer had planned to purchase Collinwood in partnership with a wealthy, elderly neighbor, Captain Westhaven. The two were scheming to get the property at a ridiculously small price, which Hampstead would pretend represented the finest offer. They intended to exploit the rich acres of timber, but Gerald Collins' occupancy of the house shattered their hopes. And so Hampstead carried out his duties as the estate lawyer with bleak reluctance.

Little was known of the new squire of Collinwood except that he spent a great deal of his time exploring distant lands for archaeological discoveries and had led one such successful expedition to Persia for the British Museum. It was also said he had a young and attractive daughter, Irma, who usually went with him on his various trips. And on this present venture in Mexico he had been joined by another member of the family, Quentin Collins.

The name of Quentin Collins was notorious in Collinsport, and the villagers heard of his association with the new squire with raised eyebrows. Quentin had been banished from the estate and the village some years before on the suspicion that he was a werewolf. Some violent attacks which were made on several townspeople had been linked to Quentin, who was said to suffer under a weird ancient curse which made him transform into a mad wolfman at certain changes of the moon.

Friends of the Collins family in the village scoffed at the charges, but the majority apparently felt them to have some basis in truth, so Quentin had been warned to leave the area. Somehow he had met Professor Gerald Collins during his wanderings and joined him on the expedition as an associate. The young man had charm and energy but was given to spells of grim rage when least expected.

Few of the people in Collinsport knew much about Mexico, thousands of miles away, and none had heard of the Quetzalcoatl. But as the stately four-masted schooner came up the Atlantic coast on its way to the Maine village the dark shadow of the curse of the flying serpent drew closer. Its horror and menace would be the most talked of and feared threat the ancient mansion of Collinwood had ever known. Within a short interval after the arrival of Professor Collins and his attractive daughter, terror would spread out from Collinwood. A loathsome monster would be unleashed on the community to kill again and again in a shocking fashion—a creature so horrifyingly ugly that the very sight of it was said to cause paralysis of its victims and even death from heart seizure.

But Professor Collins had foreseen none of this six months before in the lush jungle setting of Guardijilos where he had set up his camp to explore the site of a long-lost Aztec village. His expedition to Mexico had been crowned with success and from the ruins of the ancient village he had unearthed many items related to the culture of the early civilization along with treasures in gold and precious gems.

The expedition had been shadowed by only two things. One was the difficulty in keeping native help since many of the local people were superstitious and feared that the uncovering of the village, along with the burial places of many of its elders, might bring the curse of Quetzalcoatl upon them. It was the first time Professor Collins had heard of the ancient curse of the feathered serpent and though he did his best to persuade the hired natives that their fears were groundless, he had little influence on them.

The second problem was the difficult behavior of Quentin Collins. The professor had taken on the brilliant young man as a partner without realizing that he had a personality which made him almost impossible to work with. And when Quentin showed signs of falling in love with the professor's daughter, Irma, the problem became complicated.

On an evening in late February Irma had burst into the rough camp where Professor Collins made his headquarters. Standing in the dark shelter lighted only by a single flickering candle, she complained to her father about Quentin's unwelcome attentions.

"He refuses to take a hint," dark-haired, oval-faced Irma said. "What am I going to do?"

Her father, bald and mild-looking, listened to her story with a cloud on his sensitive face. "There is only one thing to do," he said. "I must ask Quentin to leave the expedition."

"But can you manage that at this late date?"

"I feel it must be done," her father said firmly. "Quentin doesn't get along with the workers and he constantly makes a nuisance of himself with you. He has done nothing to help the expedition and a great deal to harm it."

Irma had sensitive, fine features like her father and liquid gray eyes. These now mirrored her worry. "I'm sure he doesn't feel that way. To hear him, we would never have found the hidden village without him."

Gerald Collins frowned. "That simply isn't true. Unpleasant as the prospect is, I must face talking to him and getting all this settled."

"I think he's been doubly troublesome since you received that letter from Collinsport," Irma suggested.

Her father sighed. "I believe you're right. It seemed to upset him that Collinwood was left to me."

Her glance was knowing. "After all the awful stories he has told us about the house and the people in the village, I don't see why he should mind."

"From all that I gather, Quentin got in some serious difficulty there," her father said. "He has been vague about the details. And of course he's very vindictive."

"That's why I fear what will happen if you dismiss him from the expedition."

"Our association will not end pleasantly in any case," Professor Collins said unhappily. "Better to face up to that and get it over with."

"Would it be wiser to wait until the ship arrives and we have transported our findings to it?"

"No. Quentin keeps on quarreling with our foremen and slowing down work. We'd do better without him."

"I wish we were on the schooner and bound for Collinwood now."

Her father rose with a smile and touched a hand to her arm. "We will be soon. I hope to get on our way in another month or so."

She gave a tiny shudder. "There's something strange about the atmosphere here. And all this talk about an Aztec curse terrifies me! Perhaps you shouldn't have disturbed the ruins."

The professor said, "My dear, my whole life has been dedicated to archaeology. My single purpose is to explore the cultures of yesterday and make them understandable to our generations. The treasure we happened to have come upon in this village will not be used by me for personal gain. Most of the fine pieces will be turned over to museums and only a bare few will be sold to defray the cost of our search."

"But many of the natives consider us trespassers," she worried. "They see us as desecrating burial places. That is why you're having so much trouble finding workers."

"Pure ignorance on their part," her father said, dismissing her argument in a way that convinced her she could never get him to see things as she did. While she didn't agree completely with the natives, she could understand their feelings in the matter.

Their campsite, which was not far from the coast, was set in one of the low-lying rain forests. It was not a hospitable territory, especially for white people. The area was covered by dank marshlands and dense rain forests with trees that stretched upward to towering heights. The climate was excessively hot and humid. The Aztecs had built their cities there. They were not cities in the modern sense, but were temple centers which were used for elaborate ceremonials. Small wonder that the dark legends about strong spirits guarding such places still existed among the natives.

Irma had been on hand to see the discovery of the three small temple rooms whose walls were painted with Aztec murals. The scenes were filled with warriors, masked god-impersonators, dancers and musicians. There were a host of priests and their sacrificial victims, their hands shown dripping blood.

Her father, after clearing the floor of the third room, had found a large floor slab with finger holes in its surface to facilitate lifting. When the slab was raised it revealed a vaulted staircase that descended at a forty-five-degree angle into the rubble-packed interior of the temple's pyramid base. For days the workers slaved at clearing away the rubble.

They discovered that the stairway reversed itself and went on down in the opposite direction. At the eighteenth step down, more than fifty feet below the temple room floor, a crude stone wall blocked their way. When this was removed they found an offering of seashells, pottery, beads and pearls in a large vessel. Along the passageway Professor Collins discovered the skeletons of six individuals who had been buried with their offerings. They came to another vertically set slab of stone which, when removed, revealed a vaulted chamber thirty feet in length. Modeled in stucco relief on its walls were the figures of nine richly garbed personages.

Irma's father had roamed about the chamber and pointed out its treasures. Lantern in hand, he showed her the secrets so long kept from the view of the living. It was from this burial place that the riches of some Aztec ruler had been recovered.

Now in the candlelit shanty Irma smiled weakly at her father. "I don't share your interest in these lost worlds," she said. "I'm afraid I'm much more anxious to journey to our new home at Collinwood."

"Once we have established our home there I'll not expect you to come along on such expeditions as this again," her father assured her. "It is much too dangerous for a woman. It is also time you enjoyed society some and considered getting married."

Irma blushed. "I'm not concerned about marriage. I only want to leave this strange, haunted place."

"You shall," he promised her. "Just be patient a little longer."

Their conversation was interrupted by the arrival of a third party in the shadowed atmosphere of the shanty. Quentin Collins appeared in the doorway with a sneering smile on his rather pleasant, side-whiskered face.

"Am I intruding?" he asked.

"Not at all," Gerald Collins said. "In fact, I'm glad you've come. Irma and I have been discussing you."

Quentin gave her a quick glance. "Has your report on me not been favorable?"

Her cheeks burned again. "Why do you suggest that?"

"I do more than suggest it; I suspect it," the young man said sourly and turned to her father. "No doubt Irma has told you that I asked her to marry me?"

The professor looked unhappy. "I don't think this is either the time or place for my daughter to be considering marriage."

"Nor am I the man you want her to consider! Why not say it all?" Quentin said jeeringly.

Gerald Collins' chin jutted out. "Very well, if you insist on my being candid, I can think of others whom I'd prefer my daughter take as a husband."

"Fine!" Quentin said with a grim smile. "So you offer me honesty even if you withhold respect and friendship."

His eyes met the young man's directly. "Do you feel you have behaved in a manner to warrant my respect and friendship?"

"I've done well enough," Quentin snapped, "but you've refused to give me any credit for my efforts."

Professor Collins frowned. "I deny that. I would suggest that you leave camp in the morning. I'll see you receive a fair payment for your services to date."

"Oh, no!" the younger man protested. "You don't get rid of me that easily. I have a share of the complete find coming to me!"

"I disagree," Gerald said calmly. "Only a tiny percentage of the value of our finds goes to the group."

"That was not our agreement!" Quentin protested.

"I insist that it was," Professor Collins replied. "Now I repeat that I wish you to be ready to journey to the coast tomorrow morning."

Quentin's strong young hands clenched and unclenched as he glared at Gerald. "And if I refuse to leave?"

Professor Collins shrugged. "Then I'll refuse to vouch for your safety. You have made enemies among the workers. Several times I have interceded on your behalf. If they get the idea you are no longer under my protection I hesitate to say what could happen to you."

Quentin couldn't hide the fact that this was a disturbing ultimatum. Irma knew what her father said was true. Quentin Collins was hated by the native foremen and also by the workmen. He had abused some of them physically and never missed an opportunity to make fun of their customs and superstitions.

The flickering candlelight showed the indecision on Quentin's face. He gave Irma a sharp glance. "Do you want me to leave?" he asked.

"Yes," she said quietly. "I think it in your best interests."

"Wonderful!" he said mockingly. "You are a fine female hypocrite. You should fit in well at Collinwood. Your mealy-mouth manner should go excellently there."

Professor Collins stood between her and Quentin. "I will not have you addressing my daughter in that manner," he warned him.

"You've managed to cheat me out of my share of the treasure and get Collinwood for yourself," Quentin told him. "Don't play righteous father—it doesn't suit you."

"I don't think we have anything worthwhile to say to each other," Gerald told the younger man, "so I'll ask you to leave us. In the morning I'll see you and allot your share of earnings before you embark on your journey."

"Thank you," Quentin said with sarcasm. "And I wish you both well at Collinwood. You deserve the cursed place!" With that he wheeled around and strode out into the jungle darkness.

Irma looked at her father with dismay. "Did you see the hatred in his face? I'm afraid of what he may do!"

His sensitive face was stern. "He'll not try anything. He is dependent on me for protection from the natives. If he should harm us he'd find himself in grave danger."

She sighed deeply. "Then that will be his only reason for leaving without attempting some villainy. I don't know why you ever tolerated him."

"He came to me with a whining story about being a distant cousin and of his deep need for some worthwhile employment," her father said. "He feigned an interest in archaeology when all he was looking for was treasure. Now the mask is torn from him and we'll be rid of him."

"It can't be too soon," she said. "At least we shouldn't have to worry about him showing up at Collinwood. He seems to even hate the name of the place."

Gerald Collins nodded. "I suspect he would be afraid to go there. The authorities ordered him to leave on his last visit."

"What crimes do you think he committed?" Irma asked

fearfully.

"I have heard dark rumors—not anything I can truly believe. But it is possible he suffers some sort of madness and that at the full of the moon he becomes violently insane."

"And it is then he commits his crimes?"

"Yes. From what little I have learned he becomes a kind of crazed wolfman and attacks innocent victims as a wolf would. But these facts only came to me after I had invited him on the expedition and during my correspondence with some old friends in Collinsport."

"He probably guesses you've heard these things," Irma said.

"Without a doubt," her father agreed. "But there is no reason why you should alarm yourself unduly. He will be gone in the morning and we shall wind up matters here as quickly as possible and prepare ourselves to leave."

That night Irma returned to the camp she shared with a native woman her father had hired as her personal servant. She knew little English but could tell Irma's moods. Now she looked concerned when she saw her mistress, and made a great deal of helping Irma prepare for bed and arranging the mosquito netting above her before retreating to her own narrow cot at the other side of the shanty.

Irma tossed and turned in the humid night. The scene with Quentin had upset her and though she had her father's reassurance that the moody young man would not attempt to harm them, she still worried. She was afraid of the jungle with its snakes, lizards and other weird denizens. Even the birds filled her with awe because of their colors and variety, and the legend of the feathered serpent god handed down from the Aztecs had made a vivid and frightening impression on her.

Its name was Quetzalcoatl. It was part serpent and part bird—a great snakelike thing with feathers that enabled it to fly. Several times in the jungle when some huge bird had come swooping close to her through the thick green branches she had cowered in fear remembering the terrifying account of the feathered serpent. Of course she had never seen such a creature but the natives insisted some still remained. Some of them worshiped at temples dedicated to this serpent god.

Every sound in the jungle seemed ominously close at night, and Irma feared most of them. She had seen death come with lightning rapidity to the natives when bitten by a venomous snake or attacked by a beast of prey. The very insects could deliver death and their bite often produced grim sickness. Now, all she could think of was release from this jungle camp and a return to the safe and calm atmosphere of New England. She had never been to Collinsport or seen the family mansion known as Collinwood, but she was certain, despite Quentin's biased accounts to the contrary, that it must be a fine place.

She fell into a perspiration-drenched sleep with dreams of a cool Maine to comfort her. When morning came she joined her father at breakfast and learned that Quentin had already left the camp.

"Quentin left early," he explained. "He'll reach the safety of the coast before nightfall. He didn't relish the idea of journeying through the jungle after dark or camping in it for a night. This way he can make the trip by daylight."

Irma studied her father's weary face anxiously and asked, "Did you have a bad time with him?"

"Of course he wasn't satisfied with his share, though I was generous if anything. But he didn't say too much. There was more an implied threat in his manner. He suggested that he would meet me again one day and settle the score."

"As long as he's gone," she said.

Her father smiled ruefully. "He also suggested that you might have come to care for him except for my bad influence."

She widened her eyes. "That's pure fancy on his part. He is pleasant enough looking and can be charming when he likes, but his other side spoils all that. And to top that, there are all those rumors about him."

"I know," he agreed.

"Because I learned his true nature I couldn't ever care for him," she said.

"Probably he realizes that and it only angers him more," her father agreed. "I sent three natives along with him as guides and to carry his belongings. If he reaches the coast safely he should find a ship for transportation home in a week or so."

"I feel better just knowing that he is gone," Irma said.

"And now I must work harder than ever to finish here so we'll be able to leave on time," Gerald Collins went on.

And so there had begun a period of ten days in which her father set a frenzied pace of work to finish at the site of the excavation. Precious objects were carefully crated for transport to the coast and Irma did her share by listing everything carefully and writing down descriptions of them from her father's dictated accounts.

It seemed to her that with every passing day the jungle became more humid and menacing. She also noted sullen expressions on the faces of the natives as her father made them work harder. She also felt they disliked the idea of the many treasures being taken from the site of the ancient temple.

Irma's servant-woman, Dolores, managed in her halting English to convey to her some of the resentment that was felt. She said, "Men do not like temple idols being taken."

"But my father has respect for them," she tried to explain. "He will see they are placed in great museums and visited by our people."

Dolores showed no comprehension. "Men fear the curse of Quetzalcoatl."

Irma tried to hide her uneasiness at the mention of the serpent god. "We mean no harm to your god."

"Men think flying serpent will follow and kill them because they stole from temple," Dolores said.

"They are wrong," Irma said. "My father has not taken these things for himself or for profit. Can't you make them understand that?"

But of course the stolid woman didn't understand these facts herself, so there was little hope she would pass the information on to the others. Irma could only take comfort that every day ended meant one less than before, that they would soon follow the trail Quentin had taken through the jungle to the coast.

At last the great day arrived and they left the campsite at dawn as Quentin had. But their progress through the green forest could not be as fast as his. They were weighted down with the heavy crates of treasure, so they were forced to halt and make temporary camp in the middle of the hostile jungle. Her father was a veteran of this type of traveling and gave the natives stern instructions about setting up the camp.

Irma remained close by her father's side that night. They sat by the friendly campfire discussing what they would do on their arrival at the small coastal village where the schooner was to come and pick up them and their crates of fabulous Aztec finds.

"Juan is coming with us on the ship," he told her.

She knew Juan only by sight. He was a little white-haired man with a bronze face and serious mien. He had acted as her father's personal liaison man with the workmen during the months at the excavation.

"Why do you need Juan?" she asked.

A strange light showed in her father's eyes as he stared at the dancing flames. "I am taking back some live specimens and I need someone to be in charge of them. Juan struck me as the ideal person."

Irma was startled. "Live specimens?"

Gerald Collins smiled at her. "Yes. I have come upon some fabulous creatures this time. I'm certain they present links between animals familiar to us now and missing ones prevalent in a much earlier age so I'm selecting a certain group to take back for study."

"You've never done this before."

"I have never made such interesting finds before."

She felt an old fear returning to her. "I'm terrified of these forests and the creatures in them. I have visions of all kinds of horrible things. And some of those I've seen have lived up to my worst nightmares. I don't like the thought of your bringing them on the ship."

Gerald regarded her indulgently. "You wouldn't expect me to cater to your childish fears and rob science of an unusual opportunity? No one has brought such creatures back to civilization before."

Irma shuddered. "I wish you'd leave it to someone else."

"I can't do that," her father said. "I feel a responsibility about this. It may be years before anyone ventures as deep into these forests as we have or makes the same kind of discovery. I have no right to stand in the way of progress."

"Perhaps not," she said bleakly.

But that night as she slept by the campfire she dreamt of the flying serpent. The great thick serpent with its brightly colored plumage came descending down from the air towards her. She screamed in terror as its forked tongue writhed close to her face and she felt its fetid breath.

She came out of the nightmare really screaming. She was sitting up staring into the ebbing flames of the campfire, when her father, awakened by her cries, tried to placate her. But she slept no more that night. As dawn streaked between the towering treetops she was wide awake and tense.

Fortunately they reached the coastal village before the second nightfall and she had a clean bed in the house of one of the officials of the tiny Mexican port. She had a good rest and the next day the four-masted schooner that was to take them back to the United States came into port. The sight of it gave Irma some much-needed courage.

But she was filled with apprehensions as the loading of the cargo began. First to go into the hold of the graceful vessel were the crates of treasure. Then supplies were taken for the long voyage. After that her father began the supervision of the loading of the crates of living specimens he was taking back with them. Juan was much on hand for this and Irma, having already moved into her cabin on the ship, was also there to watch the weird collection of creatures being delivered to the schooner's deck.

Some of the crates had only air holes in them and she

couldn't see what they contained. But some had iron rungs and she was able to see the ugly lizards, birds, and crocodiles. The crocodiles with their powerful jaws, short legs, and narrow pointed heads, terrified her, though Juan insisted they were not hostile to humans. She found this hard to believe, and when the Mexican opened the top of one of the closed-in crates and revealed a veritable snake-pit, she cringed in disgust.

It was horrible. Reptiles of all sizes from a few inches to several feet long squirmed about in the bottom of the box. She saw their glittering eyes and their tongues flick in and out and watched them knot and tangle among each other. She was filled with a dreadful sensation of evil. Juan seemed amused by her revulsion.

Then one especially large box with ominous holes bored in its sides was carefully carried on board. She asked Juan what it contained. He gave her a look of grim irony.

"It is the big one," he said. "Like Quetzalcoatl." And he left her to supervise its being lowered down into the hold of the ship.

Irma stood in the glaring sunlight, staring after the descending box in alarm, not daring to believe that it could truly hold a feathered serpent. Such things no longer existed—if they ever had! She must make herself believe that!

CHAPTER 2

The voyage was destined to be a long and somewhat stormy one. It took them around Cape Horn and up the coast of South America. There were times when Collinwood and Maine seemed very far away to Irma. Her father kept busy writing a detailed account of his findings and the living specimens he was bringing back to the United States, but they had their meals together, along with Captain O'Blenis and Martin Long, the First Mate of the schooner.

Captain O'Blenis was an elderly, crotchety man given to solitude and an almost continuous study of the Bible when he was not on duty. He had a long white beard like one of the prophets in the Old Testament, for which he had an inordinate fondness and a weakness for quoting.

Smiling at her from the head of the table in the small cabin, he had said to her at their first meal together, " 'Can the Ethiopian change his skin, or the leopard his spots?' Food for thought, eh, my dear Miss Collins?"

She had been taken back by his weird manner and habit of continually quoting from the Scriptures. She would not have been able to enjoy her meals if First Mate Martin Long had not been there to balance things. Whenever the captain uttered one of his surprising quotations the red-haired young man would slyly wink at her across the table. Irma's father somehow kept up a reasonable conversation with the skipper, but the atmosphere at mealtimes continued to be strained.

Martin sought Irma out on deck after they'd been at sea a few days. It was the early evening, and although the waves were high and the ship's motion was marked, it was pleasant. Irma had been standing by the rail alone near the stern when the young man came to stand with her.

Smiling, he said, "Is it true you are afraid of the captain?"

"Not really," she said shyly. "But he does make me uneasy."

"I have watched you flinch when he begins his fire and brimstone talk and I've worried that you might end the voyage with severe indigestion."

She laughed at the young man's comment. "I didn't know my suffering was all that obvious."

Martin said, "The old man has no right to make you miserable. If he wasn't such a fanatic I'd tell him. But it would do no good."

"How did he get to be such a Bible-quoter and reader?"

"It began about three years ago," Martin Long said with a sigh. "We were docked in Sydney, Australia, picking up a cargo. The captain had some free time to spend ashore and he wound up at one of those evangelistic meetings. The preacher was a regular Bible-thumper and had a long white beard. The captain was hypnotized by him and by the way he held the crowds who came to hear him. When we left port he began his Bible-reading and grew himself a long white beard just like that famous preacher had."

"And he's been imitating him ever since?"

"That's a fact," Martin said sorrowfully. "I'm a religious man myself but this has been too much. He doesn't really care about religion. He's just putting on a show."

Her eyes were twinkling. "Don't despair. He may decide to give up the sea one day and become an evangelist."

"It would be a relief to me and all the rest of the crew and that's the truth," Martin Long said seriously.

"I won't be so frightened of him now that I know some of his history," she said. "Before you explained, I was afraid he might be going mad."

"Not a bit of it," the young man said with disgust. "He likes to draw attention to himself, and playing the part of a seagoing Moses is his way of doing it."

"Have you been at sea long?" she asked.

"Since I was a boy," Martin told her. "I've been First Mate of this ship for two years now."

"And you're still a young man," she said, impressed.

"Yes, miss," he said, seeming pleased. "It's a rare treat to have a nice young woman like you aboard. The sea can be a lonely place."

"But you do have adventure."

"I suppose so. But after a while you long for port and the sight of a pretty face, if you'll excuse the expression."

She smiled. "When you get to be captain you'll be able to marry and bring your bride aboard. I understand that many captains do."

"I would like that," he agreed, "to stay with the sea and have a wife at my side. But there's small chance of that happening unless O'Blenis goes completely daft or takes to the preaching circuit."

"I'm sure he'll tire of his talents being wasted on the crew and get hungry for a larger audience."

"That could be a happy day for all of us," Long said. "So you are going to live in Maine?"

"Yes."

"We've never sailed to Collinsport before," he said. "Though we've docked at Portland more than once. Maine is nice but cold in winter."

Irma made a face. "That doesn't bother me. I'll be glad to see some snow and feel the cold. I hated it in Mexico. All the heat, and that awful jungle. I don't want to ever be in a place like it again."

"By the time we reach Maine it will be early summer," he promised. "So you'll see it at its best."

"My father has promised to make me a home there," she said. "In the future he'll go on his expeditions alone."

"I guess that would be a lot better for you."

"It's what I want."

He frowned. "Some of the cargo we're carrying is pretty strange," he said. "I mean the livestock your father is bringing back."

She sighed. "I suppose you're talking about the snakes."

"I know about them," he said. "But there are some other creatures in those cases which they say have never been seen by white men before."

"Oh?" she lifted her eyebrows. "I hadn't heard about them."

"The crew have been talking," he confided. "Grumbling might be closer to it. They don't like some of the things down there in those cages. And they don't think old Juan is capable of looking after them all."

"He's my father's most trusted helper."

"I think he tries hard," Martin agreed, "but it's a big job trying to keep all those things alive and well for a voyage this long."

"My father must think it's possible or he wouldn't try it."

"I'd say that he hopes it is possible. And for my part I hope none of them ever gets free. Especially the Dimetrodon that old Juan told me about."

"My father hasn't mentioned it."

"He wouldn't want to upset you. They say it's a real monster, a holdover from thousands of years ago. It's a relative of the dinosaur, only a midget size compared to it, but still as large as an alligator."

She stared at him in surprise. "There's actually a thing like that alive down below?"

"Yes. And some say there's a feathered serpent down there too."

Irma gasped. "The feathered serpent is a legend. I don't believe any such thing ever existed." Still she was troubled by the memory of Juan's comment as that mysterious crate had been lowered into the hold. Had he been teasing her or telling the truth?

"Maybe you're right. But I know this Dimetrodon isn't any wild dream. Some of the crew had a quick look at it when Juan was feeding it."

"I must ask my father about it," she said.

He nodded. "I'd like to hear more about the history of that monster. I hope we don't get any really bad weather. I wouldn't want any of those crates to be broken open and those things to get loose."

The thought was terrifying. "Do you think there's any chance of that?"

Martin shrugged. "It could happen if we hit a real blow--and these waters around the Cape are right for that kind of weather."

"It's been pretty good so far."

"It has, at that," he agreed. "If we're lucky the fair spell will continue. In the meantime all you have to be afraid of is the captain."

Irma managed another smile. "He doesn't seem half so bad now you've told me about my father's cargo."

"Don't let it worry you. We'll be on the watch if bad weather should come. We'll see that you're protected."

Irma sighed. "I hope my father has plans for taking care of the collection when we reach shore. I'll be relieved to be free of them."

"I guess you've had enough of the jungle and its denizens," Martin said.

"To do me all my life."

"Nearest thing I've ever seen to a true monster was a giant sea serpent we spotted in the Sargasso Sea," he said earnestly. "It was almost as long as the ship and I was afraid its ugly head would come up over the side and it would grab one of us in its teeth."

"Did you really see such a creature?"

"Yes, miss," he vowed grimly. "I almost was ready to give up the seafaring life. I would have if I'd ever seen anything like it again. But I didn't."

"I've heard that most of the sea serpents people claim to have seen are usually long trails of thick seaweed given life by the viewer's imagination."

"If that's so what I saw was a mighty fearsome hunk of

seaweed," Long said as he tipped his cap and left her.

Irma stood alone by the railing for a few minutes. The creaking of the ship and the wash of the waves against its hull held a fascination for her. The tall masts swung against the sky rhythmically as the schooner sped on with its strange cargo. The whisper of wind that gently billowed its sails propelled it along at a good pace. Darkness was beginning to fall and she left the rail to walk ahead to the cabins occupied by her and her father.

Her father was sitting at the writing table beside his bed, his quill pen in hand as he wrote carefully in a lined ledger. Aware of her arrival, he glanced up with a welcoming smile. "Have you been out enjoying the ocean breeze, my dear?" he asked.

"Yes." She sat on the bed and took off her shawl. "I was talking to the First Mate."

Her balding father sat back in his chair. "Ah, yes, a fine young fellow. I like him."

"So do I," she agreed. "He was discussing the cargo with me. I mean the live part of it."

Professor Collins looked wary. "Ah, yes."

Irma studied him directly. "Father, you've been holding back some information from me about the things you have on board."

He cleared his throat apologetically. "I know how you feel about some of those creatures," he said. "I haven't wanted to worry you."

"I should know the truth," she reproached him. "I am here on board and a possible victim of those things if any of them should get loose."

Her father raised a protesting hand. "They are all carefully caged and crated."

"Would the cages and crates last in a really violent storm?"

"I would expect so."

"And I doubt it," she said. "And so does the First Mate."

"No one can tell until the situation arises," he said with a hint of irritation. "You're allowing yourself to be alarmed without a reason."

"I disagree," she said. "Why didn't you tell me about the Dimetrodon?"

Professor Collins registered surprise. "How did you find out about it?"

"The First Mate told me."

"He had no right to," he said, upset. "It's nothing that concerns you."

"Why did you risk bringing such a hideous monster back?"

Her father got up and began to pace the small cabin. "I couldn't not do it as a scientist," he pleaded. "This animal dates to the Paleozoic period. By some accident of nature we have this modern survival of it.

It bears no relation in size to the original creature bearing its name, but in appearance there is a strong resemblance."

"How large is it?"

He hesitated. "It is a member of the reptile family. But it is almost as large as a small horse."

Irma gasped. "I heard it was like an alligator."

"It has an alligator's scales and a reptilian head low on the ground, but its back arches up and it has a great leathery wing running down the middle of the back."

"It sounds ghastly!"

The professor looked unhappy. "I did not go to all this trouble because it is pleasant to look at. I've brought it with us because it is a true monster and may offer a link between today and thousands of years ago. Scientists of the world will thank me."

"Only if you get it to civilization safely," she warned him.

"I must do that."

"That will depend largely on fate," she said. "And what about the feathered serpent?"

Her father stared at her in surprise. "You know that is only a legend."

"Some of the crew believe you have one in one of the sealed boxes."

"There is a box with a large boa constrictor in it," he explained. "Juan has been given orders to be extremely careful of it. No doubt that is how the rumor began."

Irma studied her father with doubting eyes. He had concealed some of the truth from her and she'd found him out. How was she to know that he wasn't also lying about the feathered serpent? It was barely possible that he had come upon one of the rare monsters and decided to bring it to the United States.

"I hope you're being frank with me, Father."

He came over to her and bent and kissed her on the forehead. "You really mustn't worry. Leave that to me."

"I'll try," she sighed. "But I won't deny that I'll be glad to be rid of your collection of monsters. What do you plan to do with them when we reach Collinsport?"

Professor Collins faced her guiltily. "Well, the obvious thing, my dear."

"What do you mean?"

He spread a hand in explanation. "I'll keep them available for study."

"Where?" she asked sharply.

"Somewhere at Collinwood, I suppose. There must be stables and outbuildings, not to mention the cellars of the main house for those creatures that thrive in darkness."

A chill ran down her spine. "You mean I have to go on living with those dreadful things?"

"Until I complete my studies of them," he said embarrassedly. "Then I shall present the reptiles and rats to some zoo."

"Rats?" she repeated incredulously.

"Yes," he said, sounding enthusiastic. "A new and most interesting variety. Very fierce and larger in size than the rats we know. I'm positive we'll learn a lot from them."

"Especially if they manage to get the run of the ship," she said in a tone of awe. "It could start a panic among the crew."

"You're borrowing trouble," he told her. "No such thing will happen."

"You're going to spoil Collinwood for me," Irma declared, on the verge of tears. "I've been so looking forward to being there and now I find you're planning to fill the place with monsters."

"Only for a short time!" he pleaded.

"You don't care about me," she told him. "Your work means more to you than your daughter!"

"Quite untrue," Professor Collins declared. "But I do have a responsibility to the world of science and research. I can't deny that."

"I find you hopeless, Father." Irma rose angrily and went into her own cabin, slamming the door shut after her.

"Irma!" Gerald pleaded from the other side of the door. "Irma, allow me to explain further."

"No, Father!" she cried out and pressed the bolt to lock the door. And then she threw herself on the bunk in her cabin and gave way to unrestrained sobbing.

Her sleep that night was tormented by nightmares of the weird monsters which her father had caged almost directly beneath them in the schooner. She was pursued by the reptiles and then one of the snarling, angry rats leaped up on the bed and its tiny red points of eyes glared at her through the darkness. She screamed again and again and wakened to find it was a dream.

"Irma, are you all right?" her father's troubled voice called from the other side of the bolted door.

"Yes," she called out wearily.

"Why were you screaming?" his voice came in muffled query.

"Because of your monsters plaguing my sleep," she told him bitterly.

"I'm sorry," he said abjectly. "Is there anything I can do?"

"Let me be!" she told him.

She listened and heard him go back to his own bed. Afterwards she lay awake, conscious of every movement of the ship and its creaking. It would be weeks before the voyage would end, and she would have to endure day after day of strain. The thought of it sickened her. Only when utter exhaustion closed her eyes did she fall asleep again.

In the morning she wakened to the shouts of the crew trimming the schooner's sails. She was conscious of more motion in the ship's movements. It was almost pitching up and down on the ocean. When she ventured out on deck she found it was drizzling rain and visibility had been reduced to almost the edge of the railing. Moreover, the waves were mountainous with foam-flecked caps.

Rather unsteadily she made her way to the cabin where they had their meals. Captain O'Blenis was sitting at the table over a plate of griddlecakes and syrup. Her father was seated rather dismally at the other end of the table and the First Mate was missing. As she took her place the captain stood and bowed respectfully. Then he sat down again and began to stroke his long white beard.

"Nasty blow, Miss Collins. 'Leviathan, that crooked serpent, the dragon that is in the sea.' A dragon that has no fears for me, young woman. Not at all!"

She gazed at the latter-day prophet with some awe. "Do you think it will be a bad storm, Captain O'Blenis?"

"Who can say how the winds will blow? But this good ship will overcome all with yours truly in command. 'We went through fire and through water!' The truth lies in the Old Testament, eh, Miss Collins?"

"I hope so, Captain," she replied timidly.

Her father spoke up, "Do you consider these dangerous waters, Captain?"

Captain O'Blenis paused with his griddlecakes to stroke his long white beard and say portentously, "This has been called the graveyards of ships, sir. 'Like the driving of Jehu, the son of Nimshi. For he driveth furiously!' But you may depend on my trusty ship and crew."

"What about the livestock below?" Professor Collins murmured worriedly. "Are the crates liable to be jolted much if there is a storm?"

The patriarchal captain regarded him with scorn. "To quote Job: 'Great men are not always wise!' So I must tell you, Professor, that in the event of a storm some of your crates and cages surely must be destroyed. In short, smashed to splinters, sir!"

Collins paled. "That mustn't happen," he said miserably.

Captain O'Blenis rose grandly. "I have told you the truth. 'Who is this that darkeneth counsel by words without knowledge?' You had best be prepared for the worst, Professor Collins." And with this warning delivered he stalked out of the cabin onto the rainy deck.

Irma's father gave her a despairing glance. "I'm sure that old man is mad. He is making far too much of the weather. This is just a light blow."

"It seems more than that to me," she said.

"You must remain in your cabin no matter what happens," he warned. "Don't venture abroad if this blow continues."

She smiled bitterly. "Don't you realize your monsters will have no difficulty infiltrating my cabin if they get free?"

"It won't happen," he exclaimed nervously. "I'll go consult with Juan now. He can get some of the crew to see the crates are placed so they do not shift around."

"I wish you luck," she told her departing father.

She was still seated there by herself when Martin Long came into the cabin with his rubber coat and hat glistening with rain. He gave her a nod and called out to the cook, "Some good hot coffee, Sanders!" Then he turned to her. "Maybe we'll get a taste of that bad weather we talked about."

Irma said, "I call it bad enough now."

He took off his broad-brimmed rubber hat. "This is mild, Miss Collins. Not anything compared to a real storm."

"Then I hope we don't get one."

The cook came with a mug of steaming coffee and the First Mate took it and quaffed down some of the hot liquid at once. He took a deep breath and stared at her. "I think we may move around the fringe of the blow," he said. "You'd better pray for that."

"How are things below?"

"Pretty rough when I last took a glance down," he said grimly. "Juan was looking a couple of shades paler than usual."

"Father has gone down to see the crates are made secure."

"That won't help much," the young man said grimly and took some more of the coffee.

"Is there any danger in walking on the deck?"

"Not yet if you can manage to keep on your feet," he warned. "But later the waves could wash clean over us. We've stripped the sails and that's about all we can do except ride this out."

"Captain O'Blenis doesn't seem to be worried."

"That crazy old salt thinks he can shout out some Biblical quotation and calm the storm. It won't be that easy."

"Will you keep a watch for my father and see that he is safe?" Irma's fear showed in her voice.

"I will do what I can," he promised, putting down the empty coffee mug. "Now suppose I see you safely back to your quarters."

Irma was grateful for the offer and pressed close to the young man as they journeyed along the slippery, ocean-splashed deck. The schooner was heaving more than before and the sky above was dark with clouds. The noise of the wind almost made speech between them impossible. She looked about vainly for some sign of her father and saw Captain O'Blenis standing at the wheel. His white beard was being buffeted by the wind and he was in oilskins.

Martin Long saw her safely in her cabin and then continued on his way. Time passed and still her father had not returned. She sat on her bunk picturing him down below in the turmoil of the hold with the caged and crated monsters. She could only hope that Martin had been right and they would just feel the storm slightly as they passed around it. But at the moment the ship seemed to be helpless.

She heard loud shouting on deck but couldn't make out what was being said. She went over to the cabin porthole and peered out, balancing herself at the same time against the restless motion of the ship. She was startled to see that it had become as dark as night and it was now raining hard. It seemed her nerves could stand no more so she decided to put on her heavy cloak and try to reach the captain and have him check on her father's safety.

She threw her cloak over her flowing-skirted dress and fitted its hood on her head. Then she opened the cabin door, and bracing herself against the storm went out onto the heaving deck. Again there seemed nobody in sight. Pressing hard against the wall she inched along the wet deck. The giant, angry waves were not washing clear over the ship yet, but they were splashing up to the railings and streaking across the deck.

She was sick with fear as she tried to make her way towards the other area of the schooner. And then she halted as she saw her father appear on the deck. He was hatless and appeared to be running frantically toward her. It took her only a moment to know why. Pursuing him, with only a few feet between them, was the most horrifying creature she had ever seen! Involuntarily she let out a scream of fear.

Her father spied her from the distance and cried out a warning as he raced in her direction. The huge monster behind him had lost a little ground. It had a large reptilian head with a body like an alligator and a huge leathery wing down its back. It moved along with a reptile's slithering manner.

"Hurry!" she screamed encouragement to her father, thinking that he might reach her in time so they could retreat to the cabin and safely lock themselves in until help came. She had recognized the animal as the Dimetrodon Martin had mentioned.

Gerald Collins was only a dozen yards from her now and the monster still had not caught up with him, but then he slipped on the wet deck and fell sprawling forward with his hands held high.

Without thinking, Irma ran to help him and found herself standing above his outstretched body as the huge reptile swayed menacingly in preparation to attack her. Its tiny, glittering eyes set back in the flat head were burning with fury. Her father still appeared stunned and she was so hypnotized with terror she was unable to move. It seemed that her doom was sealed.

"Miss Collins!" The voice cried out at her elbow and she found herself roughly hurled aside. As she fell backwards she saw that it was Martin who had used this harsh means of rescuing her.

Irma looked up to see the young man facing the angry monster with a pole on which there was some kind of sharp hook. He stood moving from side to side as the monster's head swayed, waiting for the moment of attack so he could use the hooked pole to advantage.

Irma moved quickly backward and then struggled to her feet. She saw the Dimetrodon make a swift lunge at Martin, who, just as quickly, thrust the hooked pole into the scaly side of the horrible creature's head. It drew back slightly and then came forward to the attack again.

Gerald Collins had recovered and was attempting to crawl away from the reach of the Dimetrodon. But the monster was attracted by his movement and as Irma watched in terror, the reptilian head darted down and seized him in its sharp-toothed mouth!

CHAPTER 3

Irma thought that she would faint. Her screams were lost in the sounds of the storm. She saw her father's body lifted in the monster's mouth and shaken like a small animal. Martin made frantic proddings at the scaly beast in an effort to have it free her father but without success. The prehistoric beast had turned all its fury on her unfortunate parent.

Then the blast of a gun came with a faint clarity over the storm. She turned and saw Captain O'Blenis standing near her with a gun in his hands. He had apparently just fired the weapon. She glanced at the Dimetrodon again and saw that it had dropped her father to the deck. The huge monster had surely been hit in some vital place, for its eyes had lost their fury.

A moment later it slithered across the deck, and as the ship wallowed in the waves and dipped sharply to one side the great monster went over the railing. An instant later it vanished below the rough, foam-flecked waves. Now Martin went forward and picked up her father in his arms.

The captain aided her in crossing the deck and they all went to the cabins assigned to the Collinses.

Martin placed Gerald Collins on the bunk and began removing his torn coat and shirt. Irma and the captain stood by anxiously, then the First Mate looked up at them. "There seems no serious harm done. His arm was torn by the creature's teeth in several places but the cuts are not deep. Proper cleaning and bandaging will look after them."

Captain O'Blenis stroked his beard. "Then he is safe and the monster is now out of the way. And the storm is easing. To quote the Prophet Job: 'Fair weather cometh out of the North.' I think you need worry no longer, young lady."

Irma gave him a grateful look. "My father would be dead if you hadn't killed that beast."

"No more than my duty to those entrusted to my care, Miss Collins," the captain said.

Martin bound her father's wounds and she watched over him in the cabin. The motion of the ship became less noticeable as the waters calmed. Outside, the sky had cleared and it was light again. The prediction that they would safely skirt the storm had been right.

Her father stared up at her from the bunk with a sad expression. "I nearly cost us both our lives," he said.

"Don't think about it anymore," she told him.

"It's true," he went on weakly, still pale and shaken from his ordeal. "I was stubborn about bringing all those live specimens with us."

"You felt it your duty," she corrected him.

"I still think I was right," Gerald Collins said unhappily. "The damage was done when the crate holding the Dimetrodon broke. I was in the hold with Juan when it happened."

"Is he all right?" she asked anxiously.

"Yes. The monster came after me and ignored him. I decided my best bet was to make a run for the deck. Of course it followed me."

"I thought you were going to die before my eyes!"

"It was a close call," he admitted. "And when I saw you I knew how wrong I had been to venture to the deck area. I should have tried to confine the thing to the hold."

"Then both you and Juan would surely have been killed."

"Better than to expose you to the monster."

"We had help on deck. Between Martin and the captain the beast was controlled and finally killed."

Her father sighed. "Do you realize what a priceless contribution to science was lost when the Dimetrodon went over the side into the ocean?"

"You still have your other specimens."

"But it was perhaps the most valuable," he worried.

Irma smiled wanly. "Not as valuable as you. Captain O'Blenis had no choice when he fired that shot. Fortunately, he hit a vital spot first time."

"Yes," her father agreed. "I owe him a great debt."

"And the ship is a safer place for that monster being lost."

"I suppose so," he said, but his tone was still unhappy.

"Just hope that we have no more heavy storms and none of the other cases are damaged. Think what the situation might have been if either the rats or the snakes had gotten loose. We'd have had the crew in revolt."

"Transporting such cargo is bound to be a risky business," her father admitted. "But it is so important to science."

"I know," Irma sighed. "Science comes first with you —even before my safety or your own."

"That is hardly fair," he said. "It is rare that I have to make such choices."

"I notice the ones you make when you have no alternative," she said. "Perhaps this will be a lesson to you of the dangers which you exposed us to."

Her father looked up at her from his pillow. "I'm only too aware that I've risked you too much. On my next expedition I intend to journey alone. You shall remain safely at Collinwood. Now that we have a new home you must enjoy it and preside over it."

She gave him a wry glance. "I'd be more enthusiastic about that if you weren't planning to turn the place into a kind of zoo."

"But I must give the creatures study before placing them in the various zoos. I thought you understood that."

"I do now," she said. "And I'm disappointed."

"I shan't take long," he promised. "And then Collinwood will be free of all my eerie monsters and yours to enjoy as you like."

Irma was to think much about this on the balance of the long voyage up the coast of the United States. June was at hand when they reached the Bay of Collinsport, so Irma had no opportunity of seeing Collinwood from the ship as she'd hoped. Her father had explained that the mansion stood high on the cliffs above the ocean and had they arrived in daylight, they might have gotten a fine view of it.

They reached the harbor of Collinsport in the wake of the night boat which plied along the coast from Boston. They had to wait until the giant side-wheeler had unloaded its passengers and cargo before they could dock.

Irma stood in the bow of the schooner with Martin and her father and studied the blazing lights of the coastal ship. "She looks very pleasant with all her lights glowing."

Martin smiled. "She's well enough suited for the coastal

trade. But I wouldn't enjoy crossing the ocean on her. A vessel like this is much to be preferred."

"I'm sure of that," Professor Collins agreed. "In all our long voyage and in spite of the several spells of bad weather I lost only that one live specimen."

The First Mate smiled. "Put that down to good fortune as well. In a truly bad blow you'd have been in bad trouble. Most of those crates would have broken open and the ship would have been crawling with those creatures."

In an attempt to pass it off lightly, Irma said, "In which case I'm sure Captain O'Blenis would have come up with some Biblical quotation likening the vessel to the Ark."

Gerald Collins regarded his daughter with sad amusement. "Unlike Noah, I had only one of each variety of creature aboard, for the most part. Otherwise I would still have a second Dimetrodon to offer a startled world."

"We were better off to lose that one," Long said soberly. "The crew rested a lot easier though some of them are still muttering about a feathered serpent you're now supposed to have down there."

Collins looked startled. "I can't imagine how the rumor started."

"Nor can I," Martin observed dryly. "But then, sailors are always known to be superstitious folk."

"I'm sure they're wrong. My father has assured me there is no such monster among his specimens," Irma said.

A strange expression came over Martin's face. "Yes, miss," he said quietly. "If you'll both excuse me I must attend to getting us docked now that the night boat is moving out into the bay."

"I sometimes don't know what to make of that young man," Gerald Collins said nervously when he had left.

"He has been very good to us during all the voyage."

"Agreed," her father said hastily. "I only wish he wouldn't get such queer ideas."

She gave her father a sharp glance. "And he is wrong, isn't he?"

"Of course," her parent replied as he turned his attention to the lights of the distant coastal ship. "What an impressive sight she makes as she moves away."

"Yes," Irma said, still worried by his hint of evasiveness, though she felt she must believe in what he'd said.

She looked in the direction of the wharf with its blazing torches and lanterns standing out against the darkness and said, "We'll soon be setting foot in Collinsport."

"And about time," her parent remarked.

"There seems to be a good many people gathered on the dock," she said.

"Bound to be at this time when the night boat arrives."

"Will you unload all the cargo tonight?"

"I don't believe we'll attempt to unload anything," he replied. "We'll even remain aboard ourselves until the morning. It would be silly to make the trip to Collinwood tonight. It is several miles and very late."

"I suppose you're right," she said, though she had been hoping to leave the ship at once.

There was much shouting between ship and shore as the schooner moved in to dock. The guide lines were tied fast and they were safely beside the wharf. From her vantage point on deck Irma was able to study the movement in the area of the torch-lit wharf. A number of those who had come in their carriages to meet the night boat had already driven off. Now there were only the dock workers and a small knot of males of mixed ages studying the big schooner with interest.

Professor Collins peered into the darkness beyond the wharf. "If I remember correctly, the main street leading to the wharf is very steep with small shops on either side of it."

"You were here once before, then?"

"Yes. As a boy. But I don't remember more than a few details of the place," her father said.

They were still standing there talking when a young man came up to them with hat in hand. "My name is Stuart Jennings," he introduced himself, "and I have come aboard to welcome you to Collinsport."

Gerald Collins at once shook hands with the youth and introduced him to Irma. She liked meeting the tall, fair-haired young man. He had a friendly manner and a pleasant smile.

"My father is in the shipbuilding business," he said, "and for years he has been buying lumber from the Collins estate."

"Very interesting," Mr. Collins said. "I understand we have a great many acres of standing lumber on Collinwood land."

"You do," the young man answered. "My father also has holdings of his own, which actually adjoin your property." Then he turned to Irma. "Are you taking a carriage to Collinwood tonight, Miss Collins?"

"No," she told him. "Father thinks we should wait until morning, and there is a valuable cargo to discharge, a portion of it live animal specimens."

Stuart Jennings showed surprise at this. "I had no idea you were interested in that phase of research," he told her father.

"It is a by-product of my archaeological studies," he said. "I felt I could not ignore the opportunity to bring back some of the more interesting species."

"And where will you keep them?" the young man wanted to know.

"Temporarily at Collinwood," Professor Collins said. "When I have finished my studies I'll distribute them among various zoos."

"You'll create a lot of interest in the village," Stuart Jennings assured him. "Anything that happens at Collinwood is a subject of gossip here."

"It's not all that important," her father said brusquely.

"Perhaps not," Jennings said. "But so little happens here that any new project is bound to get attention."

"I would prefer to avoid such attention."

"Then let us hope it works out that way," Jennings said. "And if I may I'd like to drop by Collinwood in the morning and see if there is anything I can do to help you get settled in your new home."

"Thank you," Irma said politely.

"That is good of you," her father said. "I shall be kept here at the dock until all the cargo is removed. But my daughter can go on ahead."

Stuart smiled at her. "In that case I may as well come directly here to the wharf in my carriage and escort you to Collinwood."

"It would be far too much trouble," she protested.

"Not at all," he said. "I'd consider it a privilege." And so it was settled between them that he would come for her at nine the following morning. Jennings bade them goodnight and walked off into the shadows of the deck, leaving a definite impression with her. She felt he could well be her first friend at Collinwood.

Her final night aboard the schooner was uneventful. She rose early the next morning to put the last things in her trunks and have breakfast, but before going to her final meal on the schooner she went to the ship's rail to study the wharf and the village beyond.

The gray timbers of the dock were already buzzing with activity. The crew of dock workers were beginning to remove the crates and packing cases from the ship. And she saw that the main street of the village did indeed slant down to the wharf steeply. One-story buildings clustered on either side of it and there was no sign of anyone moving in that area yet.

Her father was already at the table with Captain O'Blenis and Martin when she joined them for breakfast. There was an air of relaxation at the table. They were all glad to have the voyage completed successfully.

Her father cleared his throat to say, "My daughter and I both greatly appreciate your hospitality and interest during the long voyage."

Captain O'Blenis looked pleased. "A voyage we all shall remember. 'He maketh the deep to boil like a pot.' But fortunately the storms were not as bad as they could have been."

Irma and the First Mate finished breakfast first and left the table together. She said goodbye to the white-bearded old captain and then went out on deck with Martin.

Shyly she asked, "Will I be seeing you again?"

His expression was solemn. "No, Miss Collins, I expect not. As soon as we are rid of your father's cargo the captain wants to set sail at once for Boston."

"I had hoped you might remain here a few days."

"So had I," he agreed. "But the captain is in a hurry to find another cargo, and Boston is the best port near here for loading."

Her eyes met his earnestly. "I do thank you for everything. And if you come by this way again do look up my father and me. The name of the estate is Collinwood."

"I won't forget, Miss Collins," he promised.

She extended a slim hand to him. "I've enjoyed our friendship."

"So have I, miss," he said, taking her hand in his huge calloused one.

When he let her hand go, she said, "I must return to my cabin and make sure I have everything packed. A young man is calling to take me to Collinwood in his carriage."

Martin smiled. "Yes, miss. I met him last night. In fact I directed him to where you and your father were standing talking."

Irma blushed a little. "Really? Then you can tell him I'm ready when he comes," she said as she hurried off to her cabin.

It was a half-hour later when Stuart Jennings arrived. He knocked on her cabin door lightly and when she opened it, he again addressed her with his hat in hand. "Your friend, Martin Long, told me where to find you," he said. "Are you all packed?"

"Yes." She had put on a prized summer dress of light gray silk and wore a Lambelle hat of fancy straw.

Stuart Jennings studied her with open admiration. "You really look stunning this morning."

"Thank you," she said with a smile. "Most of my good things are packed."

"The First Mate has promised to send men here at once to help with your luggage," the young man said. "Some things can come in the carriage with us and the rest can be sent along by wagon."

"Fine," she said and pointed to her personal bag and a small trunk. "Can they go along with us?"

"No trouble at all," he told her with a bow. A moment later he summoned some sailors to come for her luggage. Her father was on hand to bid her goodbye but was plainly still involved in his own affairs. He was now mostly worried about getting enough wagons to move the load of cargo to the distant estate.

Irma gave First Mate Martin Long a final smile of goodbye and then made the long-anticipated transfer from the ship to land without actually thinking about it. Within a few minutes she was riding up the steep main street in the carriage with Stuart Jennings by her side. His coachman, perched on the seat ahead, was handling the team of matched gray horses with ease.

"It's a small town but a fairly lively one," Stuart Jennings told her.

"It's very quaint," she said, taking in the rather ramshackle store buildings. "And after the jungle it is very welcome."

Jennings was looking at her with twinkling eyes. "I can tell that you are not fond of the primitive life."

"Not that primitive," she said with a sigh.

"You haven't met Lawyer Hampstead yet, of course."

"No, but Father had a number of letters from him. What sort of man is he?"

Jennings suddenly looked wary. "I'd rather you decide that for yourself. There is no doubt he'll show up here soon enough. He's an elderly man and extremely sharp in business. I have an idea he may have wanted to get his hands on Collinwood for himself."

"Oh? Then he'll be disappointed that Father didn't decide to sell the property?"

"That could be," he said. "But of course I may have it all wrong."

She saw that they were leaving the main area of the village and coming onto a country road with scattered farmhouses. "You and your father must have been friends of the late owner of Collinwood," she suggested.

"We were," Jennings agreed. "Your uncle's death was a grievous shock to the community. But that was some time ago."

"Yes. It has taken us ages to get here."

Stuart smiled and said gallantly, "May I say that your arrival was worth waiting for."

She flashed him a smile. "That is very nice of you."

"Merely the truth," he said, as the carriage turned into a narrower road fringed by trees on each side of it. "We are now taking the shore road that follows directly along the cliffs to Collinwood," he announced.

"Will we have a view of the ocean?"

"Yes," he said. "We'll come to a section where there is no growth of trees on the ocean side of the road shortly."

"I'm getting excited," she said. "What sort of place is Collinwood?"

He smiled as the carriage jogged along. "That's a rather broad question," he said. "I think you will grow to like it though it may seem too large at first—it has forty-odd rooms."

Panic crossed her pretty face. "Whatever will we do with all that space?"

"You'll likely find it useful," he replied. "Most of the other owners have. There are the attic rooms used mostly for storage. Then on the floors below are the guest suites of one to three rooms each. And on the second floor are the rooms used by the family as quiet sleeping quarters with the main living room. The other general rooms are on the ground floor. At the rear of the building on each level there are certain rooms reserved for the servants."

"Then we do have some servants?" she said with relief.

"Of course, with a house that size you must," Stuart Jennings said. "So you can understand there is not that much extra space after all."

"I still like a small house."

"In which case you'd probably prefer the old house. It was the first Collinwood built when the family came to Collinsport. It's a distance back from the sea and not far from the new Collinwood."

"It sounds interesting."

Jennings frowned. "But I wouldn't count on using it. It has been reserved for years for the use of Barnabas Collins when he cares to pay a visit."

"Barnabas Collins?" The name meant nothing to her.

Stuart nodded. "You've never heard of him?"

"No."

"Your family has always had a Barnabas Collins. From the time the first Barnabas Collins left here long ago to live in England the line has always boasted a Barnabas. Many of them have visited here. I met the present Barnabas Collins two years ago."

"What is he like?"

"Charming but rather strange in manner," the young man said with a look of concentration. "He is a good talker but dresses in a quaint fashion. It is remarkable but all these descendants look exactly like the original Barnabas whose portrait hangs in the reception hall at Collinwood."

"Why did he leave Collinwood and go to England?" The wheels of the carriage creaked on, raising dust from the narrow road.

"That is a story in itself," Stuart said. "He left here under a cloud. Some people claimed he was cursed by a woman called Angelique and became a vampire. I have never been able to get two versions of the story that were the same."

She stared at him. "What exactly do you mean by vampire?"

Stuart looked uneasy. "One of the living dead. They sleep by day and travel abroad by night. And they manage to continue living by robbing the live of their blood. Especially are they fond of the blood of young women. It is the female throats which are most often pierced by their fangs."

Irma stared at him in mild horror. "You sound as if you believe it?"

"I'm afraid I do."

"I don't follow you," she said.

"The Barnabas I've met is a gaunt, handsome fellow. When he was here for a few weeks last year, several girls were attacked and left in a stunned state with fang marks on their throats. The superstitious blamed Barnabas for bearing the family curse and exerted great pressure to get him to leave. He did but I preferred to think of him as innocent. He was no more than eccentric."

She was interested. "So while you believe generally that vampires do exist you don't think the present Barnabas Collins is one?"

"That's about it."

"But many people do suspect him of being tainted with the curse?"

"Yes."

"In that case is he liable to come back?" she wondered.

"I think so," the man on the carriage seat at her side said. "They always have done so. Some kind of provision was made in a long-ago will leaving that house to Barnabas and his descendants for their use."

"So there is nothing I can legally do about taking it over?" she said. "Or that my father can do?"

"No," Stuart said. "You would be wise to forget the old house except to visit it if Barnabas should arrive again. You'd find it a beautiful old building, and although not large it has an unpreposessing exterior."

They had come to the section of the road where the trees gave way to the ocean. Irma was thrilled by the magnificent view of the water from the road which followed the curves of the cliffs high above the shore.

"It's breath-taking!" she gasped.

"The high point is a spot called Widow's Hill," he told her. "You can walk to it from Collinwood."

"It's an ideal location," she said as they turned on the narrow road.

"And there is Collinwood directly in front of us," Stuart announced.

She had her first look at the somewhat grim, sprawling mansion with its dark hulk dominating the cliffs. It was larger than she imagined and it had at least a half-dozen chimneys stretching up to the blue sky.

"I'm glad to have my first look at it in daylight," she said.

"And I'm happy to share the moment with you," Stuart told her, his hand exerting a slight pressure on hers.

"Strange," Irma said in a subdued voice. "It doesn't strike me as a happy house."

"Is any house a completely happy one?"

"But this is different!" she protested.

"In what way?" Stuart's young face was serious.

She glanced at him. "From the moment I first saw it I've had the feeling that it is grim and forbidding."

"But why?"

She shrugged. "No logical reason. It just seems to have flashed that message to me. Is it as gloomy as I fear?"

Stuart showed uneasiness. "There are mixed feelings about it."

Her eyes fixed on him. "Go on."

He hesitated. "I don't want to turn you against the place."

"Please go on!" Irma implored.

"Well," he said unhappily. "As I told you before. Like any old house, it has seen happy times and bad ones."

"And?" She was sure there was some gruesome story and she wanted to hear it.

"A few people claim Collinwood is haunted."

"Yes?"

"There have been a few murders here or near here over the years," Stuart said. "The ghosts of some of those victims are said to haunt the place. Then there is the problem of Barnabas."

"You have put that down to superstition," she reminded him.

"I still do, whatever went on in the past."

"And?" She felt there had to be more.

Stuart regarded her worriedly. "Haven't you heard enough?"

"You're still holding something back," she accused him.

"Very little," he said. "There is Quentin."

"Quentin?" The name sent a chill through her. "The Quentin Collins we had on the expedition with us for awhile?"

"I suppose it's the same one," he said with a frown. "I didn't know about that. So Quentin was with you."

"Yes. He didn't work out at all. My father had difficulty with him and had to send him back before the expedition ended."

"That sounds like Quentin," the young man said. "Then I don't have to fill you in on him. He's been back here several times and thrown a werewolf scare into the place."

"Couldn't you guard against that in some way?" she asked.

"No," he said. "Every time he's come back he's somehow fooled us. We've never realized he was around until it was too late."

CHAPTER 4

Not even a warm greeting from the housekeeper at Collinwood, Mrs. Branch, made Irma completely happy. She paused in the entrance hall of the mansion to study the fine painting of the first Barnabas Collins that hung there. She admired the face she saw and thought that if the present Barnabas looked at all like the portrait he must be a fine man.

"He was handsome," she said to Stuart.

"True," the young man agreed. "And so is the present holder of the name."

They moved on from room to room and she had to agree that the large main rooms of the house were charming. But there still lingered that something in the atmosphere of the place that worried her.

Mrs. Branch showed her upstairs to her bedroom overlooking the ocean. It was a fine room with gold drapes and a matching gold-colored satin spread on the bed. The other furnishings were elegant, including a dark maroon Persian rug which covered most of the hardwood floor. When the housekeeper left them after seeing the luggage safely installed, Irma went over to the window to admire the view of the water.

Then she turned to Stuart, who was standing in the center of the room, and with a wry smile said, "I know there isn't a reason in the world why I shouldn't love all this and yet I have this feeling of uneasiness."

"I'm sure it will pass," he said.

"Perhaps," she said quietly, staring out at the ocean again.

"You tricked me into telling you too much of the dark side of the house's history," he went on. "So you don't get a fair picture."

She looked at him with a sad expression on her lovely face. "Of course you're right. I must make up my mind to be happy here."

"I'm certain you can be."

Irma went over to him. "Thank you for your kindness. You can't imagine how much it has meant."

Jennings seemed troubled. "I'm beginning to think I've done a rather poor job."

"Not at all. My mood is my own fault," she said earnestly, "and I'm going to fight it."

"That's all it needs," he agreed. "Now that you've seen something of the house and have your things here, I guess I'm no longer needed."

"Don't feel that way about it," she implored him.

He smiled. "You do want to unpack and I can call on you at some other time."

"I hope you will," she said.

"I fully intend to—and soon. Now if you'll excuse me..." He left the room and went downstairs, Irma following closely at his heels. In the hallway he picked up his hat and turned to her again. "I trust you will come to be happy here," he told her.

"Thank you," she said quietly as she saw him to the steps, but when she closed the door after this new-found friend she felt extremely desolate. Happily she had enough to keep her occupied until her father appeared with the first of a number of wagonloads of treasure. He was so busy directing the unloading of the carts that he hardly appeared to be conscious of the vast house.

Irma remained in the background as he assigned the crates to certain areas. She was glad that some of the animals were being sent to the stables but she was upset and frightened to learn that he planned to keep most of the reptile species in the dark cellar under Collinwood with Juan as their custodian.

She complained to her father, saying, "I don't want those awful things in the house."

"But they will do no harm here!" He sounded surprised.

"That's what you say," she observed unhappily.

"Just for a little," he pleaded. "Juan is here to see that there are no problems. He is completely reliable."

Her eyes met his with reproach as she reminded him,

"Remember what happened on board the ship."

He paled slightly. "That can't happen again!"

"How can you be so sure?"

"There is no stormy ocean here to destroy the cases for one thing," he argued.

"There can be other accidents," she warned.

Professor Collins was in a stubborn mood. "You're merely trying to create trouble that doesn't exist," he said. "The specimens must remain here for a short time."

"Very well, Father," Irma said gravely. "So this is the fine home you have promised me for so long. Now I learn what it amounts to."

Her father came close to her. "You mustn't say such things. You know how much you mean to me, how I long for your happiness."

She nodded. "But it is the old story. Your work comes first. I don't even have a full knowledge of what you have in those crates. I only saw a few of them being readied for the ship."

"Harmless specimens," he said vaguely.

"Like the Dimetrodon?"

"That was different," he protested.

"At least it gave me an idea of the lengths to which you will go in the name of science," she said with resignation.

She finally tired of watching the unloading of the crates and decided to explore the grounds. She strolled along a path at the cliffs edge to the high point of ground Stuart Jennings had described as Widows' Hill. Then she took a roadway past the outbuildings and the stables to reach the old house. She knew it the moment she saw it. Thick vines grew on its dull red brick walls and its dark green shutters were all closed. It gave the appearance of a house deserted.

Something impelled her to mount the several steps to the entrance of the old house and rap on the door. Of course there was no reply. She hadn't expected one since Stuart Jennings had explained the house was only in use when the present Barnabas Collins visited. She remained there for a few moments longer and then turned to go down the steps and walk back to Collinwood.

But when she did so she was faced by the spectacle of a strange-looking old man standing a short distance from the house studying her. He was short and stocky with an immense sloppy stomach and he wore a shapeless dark coat and shabby soft hat with round top and battered brim.

His face—one which wouldn't be quickly forgotten— bore a scowl. His nose was long and prominent; he had shaggy white eyebrows over suspicious eyes and deep lines at his mouth; and his lower lip protruded over his upper one to a noticeable degree. It was hard to judge his age but she suspected he must be very old.

Leaning on his knobby walking stick, he asked in a wheezy voice, "Are you the daughter of the new owner?"

Startled, she nodded. "Yes."

The old man chuckled mirthlessly. "Do you think I'm some kind of ghost standing here in the afternoon sunlight?"

"No, but you surprised me," she said as she came slowly down the steps.

The squat old man hobbled nearer to her. Pointing a stubby finger at her, he said, "Were you hoping to find Barnabas?"

"I wondered if he might have returned."

A sour smile crossed his ancient face. "He hasn't been here lately. Maybe he won't ever come again. There are many would rest happier if that were so."

She stared at him. "May I ask who you are?"

"You may," he said sarcastically. "I am your neighbor, Captain Westhaven, retired. And if you and your father hadn't decided to come here, I and my friend, Lawyer Hampstead, would have bought this property."

He said this in a tone that indicated he believed he and the lawyer had been badly treated in not having a chance to buy up the property at a bargain price. She could see that this was a neighbor who would not wish them well. He would lose no sleep over any problem they might have getting Collinwood in order again.

She said, "I'm sorry you were disappointed."

"What do the two of you want this place for?" the old man demanded in a querulous fashion.

Irma spoke up boldly. "It was left to us and we want to make it our home."

"It's too big for two people!"

She raised her eyebrows. "Then why did you and this lawyer want it?"

Captain Westhaven's mouth dropped open. It was a question he hadn't been expecting. Glaring at her, he said lamely, "We were going to buy it as an investment in woodland. Hampstead has a sharp eye for timber."

"Then he should be able to advise my father well, since he is the estate lawyer," she said.

The captain seemed to have lost interest. He hobbled on past her, muttering to himself in a voice so low she couldn't understand him. She watched his macabre, bent figure vanishing over the hill and felt relieved to see him go.

Irma had had enough of being on her own and hurried back to the old mansion. She met Mrs. Branch in the hallway and she quickly told her of her eerie meeting with the elderly man.

"Has he a right to trespass on our land?" she asked.

"He has not," Mrs. Branch declared. "But he makes rules for himself."

"I gathered he was that type."

"People let him get away with things because he's an old man and has a lot of money. But in the five years I've worked here I've seen him get steadily worse. If you were to step on a foot of his land and he saw you he'd put a bullet in you, yet it is fine for him to come over here as he likes."

"That's what I felt was going on," she said. "When my father is less busy I'll discuss this with him."

Mrs. Branch leaned forward confidentially. "And be sure and tell him that Captain Westhaven is no gentleman. He has a criminal past."

Irma felt a chill of fear pass over her. "Are you certain?"

"Yes. I heard my late husband speak of it, rest his soul!"

"What sort of criminal past does Captain Westhaven have?" she questioned.

Mrs. Branch sounded nervous. "I can't say right out, but I know it to be true. You could ask Lawyer Hampstead. He'll be able to tell you."

"I will, then," she said.

The woman's eyes mirrored her anxiety. "But don't bring me into it," she said in a troubled voice.

"I won't if you don't want me to," she said. "You needn't worry."

"It's best that way," the housekeeper explained as she left by way of one of the long shadowed corridors that divided the house into so many sections.

Irma was left wondering at this mysterious conversation. It seemed that life at Collinwood was not going to be the placid, enjoyable existence she'd pictured. They had arrived to face hostility.

She was still considering this and other things when her father entered the front door. He was directing several straining workers in carrying upstairs a huge crate with airholes bored at intervals in its sides.

She stared at her father in disbelief. "Why are you sending that crate upstairs?" she asked him.

Gerald Collins looked uneasy. "Some of the specimens will do better in the open air. I'm having them taken to the rooftop where there is a Captain's Walk."

"What sort of specimens need to be up there?"

He sighed. "I wish you wouldn't doubt my judgment so. I

have some very unusual birds, for one thing."

Irma was upset. "I dislike every corner of this house being converted into a zoo."

"Come now," he placated her, "it's not all that bad. A few crates in the cellar and a couple on the rooftop. The rest of them are to be in the stables and outbuildings."

"You had more than a few crates placed in the cellar. I watched."

"Only a few crates of livestock," he explained. "The other boxes I sent down there contain the treasures which I must examine, document and evaluate during the next few months. Only in that way can I tell what the expedition accomplished."

"You always have some ready explanation, Father," she said with unhappy resignation.

He came across to her in the shadowed hallway. "You must concentrate on the rest of the house. You'll have plenty to occupy you in learning to take charge of it successfully."

"And you will get rid of these live specimens as soon as you can?" she implored.

"I promise."

"I hate having them here! They remind me of all the horror of that dark jungle!"

Her father patted her arm. "I understand and I'll not keep you under this strain a moment longer than is necessary."

Despite her father's promise, Irma looked on with disapproving eyes as several other crates were taken up to the rooftop. Her father had claimed he had exotic jungle birds among his specimens, and she remembered Quetzalcoatl and hoped there was no loathsome feathered serpent in the collection.

The task of moving in was completed late in the afternoon. The last of the empty wagons rolled back to Collinsport and her father began to take some stock of the great mansion which he'd inherited.

Standing with her on the lawn before Collinwood, he said, "I had only a vague remembrance of what it was like. I was only a boy when I was here. It all seemed very different."

"There is the fish packing plant in town as well," she said. "According to Mrs. Branch, the family firm sends salted fish all over the world."

"There must be a manager equipped to take care of that," he said, "and also someone to look after the farming and lumbering operations."

"I imagine so," she agreed. Glancing up at Collinwood, she added, "It is a fine mansion."

"Far too large for us," he said. "But we can somehow

manage."

"You need a great deal of room for your expedition finds," she reminded him.

"That is true."

"I find it somewhat gloomy," Irma admitted. "From the moment I first set eyes on it I've had a strange feeling that it holds many secrets—that perhaps not all of them are pleasant."

Her father smiled at her fears. "You are far too sensitive."

"I can't help it," she protested. "This has the grim air of a haunted house."

"I'm sure this is all your imagination."

"Perhaps," she said. "But we aren't going to be received with open arms by everyone here. I've at least learned that with certainty. For one thing Quentin is well-remembered in the village and blamed for some atrocious attacks on several of the local people. For another, I know that local interests hoped we wouldn't come here and they'd be able to purchase the property cheaply."

"How can you know all this?" he asked with amazement.

"I've talked with several people," she said. "Stuart Jennings told me about Quentin Collins and also our cousin from England, Barnabas. I heard about the plan to buy our property from a neighbor, a weird old man of wealth, Captain Westhaven. He and our lawyer wanted Collinwood for themselves, and Mrs. Branch assured me in strict confidence that Captain Westhaven has some kind of criminal record."

Her father was surprised as one might expect of a man so wrapped up in research that he was almost completely out of touch with the world around him. "I find all you've said utterly incredible."

"I think you'd be wise to accept it as fact," she said bitterly. "And where is Lawyer Hampstead? He hasn't been here yet to welcome us."

Gerald Collins looked confused. "I expect him momentarily, but I just can't believe that he was involved in any scheme to try to separate us from this inheritance."

"The old man I talked to was very frank about it."

"For all you know he may be mad!"

"I'd guess that he was slightly mad," she agreed, "but it is a sly kind of madness that would not deter him from taking part in such a scheme."

Professor Collins placed his hands behind his back and frowned out at the sea. "You seem to take a delight in looking at everything in the most pessimistic manner."

"No. That isn't so."

He gave her a sharp glance. "Then why bring me all this

unpleasant news?"

"So that you may be prepared."

"What was it you heard said about Quentin?"

"Only what we already know to be true. That he is a shifty, reckless person capable of acts of violence. The villagers here hate and fear him."

"We also want nothing more to do with him."

"But our name is Collins and so is his," she pointed out. "He is a member of our family, so people are bound to connect us in their minds."

Gerald sighed deeply. "I suppose that is true."

"It will take time to let them know us and understand that we are different."

"Agreed," he said.

"And if this Lawyer Hampstead and Captain Westhaven are anxious to have us out of here they'll probably do all they can to spread ugly rumors about us. That is one of the chief reasons I worry about these live specimens you've brought back."

"I don't follow you."

She gave him a wise look. "You must remember how superstitious the crew were when we made the voyage here. There were all kinds of stories about the monsters you had in those crates. The villagers could easily begin the same rumors here."

"I doubt it."

"They saw the cargo being unloaded and some of them manned the wagons that brought the crates here. They are bound to be curious. They'll have asked some questions of the crew and I'd be willing to bet they received the right answers to build on their ignorance and superstitions."

Alarm crossed her father's face for the first time. "Do you honestly believe that?"

"Yes."

"I must talk to Juan," he said uneasily. "He should have some idea if there was any gossip."

"His English is so poor he'd probably not realize," she warned.

"It is important that people understand my research is purely of a scientific nature and nothing to be feared."

"Making them understand, in the face of ugly rumors, could be an impossible task," she said. "I'm afraid it is not going to be easy for us here."

"I refuse to think that," he retorted. "And what did you hear about this Barnabas?"

"We'll have to reconcile ourselves to sharing the estate with him. His branch of the family were long ago given the right to use the old house. The present Barnabas Collins has made a series of visits here."

Gerald looked concerned. "I hope he is not the same type as Quentin."

"I think not," she said. "Most of the reports I've had seem to be favorable though he has been linked to some gossip about his ancestor. It seems the original Barnabas Collins was driven from the area because he was a suspected vampire."

"One of the dead who walk at night!" the professor observed with a low whistle. "You'll be converting me to your belief that this is a haunted house. I can hardly call this talk of monsters and vampires healthy."

"That is why I fear new rumors could easily gain ground," she explained. "The local people already look on Collinwood with superstition."

"I can't change my plans now," he said.

"So it seems, but you should be prepared for trouble."

"You spoke of the present Barnabas being linked to gossip about his ancestor," her father commented. "Do you have any idea why?"

"Not really," she said.

Gerald Collins looked unhappy. "He's probably another difficult character like Quentin. I hope he doesn't come here again."

"It would seem likely that he will."

"At least we can hope that he doesn't arrive until we have fully settled into the house," he said.

"When we go inside I'll show you the portrait of the original Barnabas in the reception hall," Irma said. "I'd call it a strong face."

Her father stared at her. "You seem oddly well-disposed toward this man whom you've never met. What is the explanation for that?"

She considered for a moment, a wistful expression on her own face. "That is strange," she admitted. "I can't really say why. Again, it is just a feeling."

"You should beware of this reliance on impressions. It could involve you in serious difficulty."

Irma knew what her father said was true, but she still felt the same way about Barnabas Collins. Perhaps it was because Stuart Jennings' comments had been largely favorable about her British cousin. Unlike her father, who had openly announced he hoped Barnabas would not appear at Collinwood again, she wished that he might come. She was positive that she would like him.

It was very late in the afternoon when a light carriage drawn by an ancient horse and with a tall, spare man in its single seat drove up to the entrance of Collinwood. Irma saw the carriage arrive from a window of the living room and at once assumed this must be Saul Hampstead finally coming to call on them.

She hurried down to the study, where her father was at work at a broad desk and told him, "We have a caller. I think it must be Lawyer Hampstead."

Annoyed at being interrupted in his work, Professor Collins rose and said sternly, "It would seem he could have waited until tomorrow rather than arrive so late."

"You still have a while to talk with him until the dinner hour," she said. "And perhaps he'll stay for dinner."

"Perhaps," her parent sighed. "Well, let us go meet the fellow!"

Mrs. Branch had already opened the door to the caller, and at closer view Irma was startled by his strange appearance. He was fully six feet tall with a bald head fringed at the ears and back with strands of iron-gray hair. His face was long and cadaverous with deep-set shadowed eyes that seemed to be continually staring with an apprehensive expression. His nose was short and snubbed, giving his high-cheeked countenance more the appearance of a skull's head than anything else.

He extended a bony hand to her father and said, "I am Saul Hampstead. Welcome to your new home and our village."

"Thank you," Gerald said, shaking hands with this fantastic-looking character. He turned and introduced her, "This is my daughter, Irma."

Hampstead offered her his bony hand and revealed a toothy smile which completed his resemblance to a skull head. "Charmed," he said in a thin, high voice.

"Won't you come into the living room," Gerald said. Within a few minutes they were all seated stiffly in the big formal room. Irma was trying to decide whether the lawyer was miserly as well as ugly and came to the conclusion he must be very mean. Nothing else could explain his threadbare dress since he must have an excellent practice.

"Do you think you will be happy here?" Hampstead wanted to know, his frightened eyes moving from one of them to the other.

"It is too soon to be sure," Gerald said, "but I think we'll find it pleasant."

"And you, Miss Collins?" The lawyer was studying her closely.

She managed a wan smile. "It is different from what I'd

expected but I agree with my father. We'll probably grow to like it."

"I see." The skull's head lost its tentative smile and in his thin voice Hampstead continued, "If by any chance you weren't impressed I'd still be happy to take the property off your hands."

"I considered your previous offer," Professor Collins said, "and found it small. Also I'd prefer to live here."

"Much of the lumber land is depleted," Hampstead said sadly, "and there is currently a dispute with the Jennings family as to boundaries. Their land adjoins yours. So my associate and I felt that the offer we made you was quite fair."

Irma spoke up. "Your associate is Captain Westhaven?"

"Indeed, he is. But how could you know that, having just arrived?"

"I met him," Irma said with just a hint of contempt in her tone. "He was strolling near the old house."

"Ah, yes," Hampstead said carefully. "He is a very old man and rather eccentric, but he has a sharp mind."

"I gathered that," Irma said. "I realized that he was trespassing but I suppose he is used to doing that."

The lawyer looked uncomfortable. "He is an old man and one of great wealth. At his age he is used to doing as he pleases. I'm sure he's never given a thought to the fact he was on your land without permission."

"As long as he allows us the same privilege," she said.

"Exactly," the lawyer replied uneasily. "Captain Westhaven has a long career behind him."

Irma said, "What sort of shipping was he involved in?"

Hampstead cleared his throat. "I'm not able to say, exactly, but it must have been extremely profitable. He has amassed a great fortune."

Irma thought this less than a satisfactory answer, but she did not pursue the subject. Instead she sat and listened while her father and the lawyer discussed the business of the estate. It appeared that it was in only fair shape. Lumber prices had been low but were on the rise, and the fishing end of the family business had been hurt by a bad season in which the catch had been lean.

Gerald Collins heard this out, saying, "But all in all the prospects are good."

Hampstead smiled coldly. "Who can predict the future?"

"Very true," her father said quietly. "We have only had a single meal here ourselves but the cooking seems excellent. Can we persuade you to remain with us for the evening meal?"

Hampstead smiled. "How kind of you, I shall be delighted to join you."

Irma was not surprised at his acceptance. She had decided

he was dreadfully mean and the prospect of gaining himself a free meal was one which he obviously could not turn down.

She rose from her chair eager to get away from his unwelcome presence. "I'll let Mrs. Branch know we're having a guest."

"Of course," her father agreed.

"This is very kind of you. I must tell you something of the legends of the house at dinner. You should hear about Collinwood's ghosts," the lawyer said.

Irma couldn't hide her distress. "Its ghosts?" she echoed.

"There are many of them," he said slyly.

CHAPTER 5

The candles, in elaborate silver candlesticks, had burned low. Dinner was over but they remained seated at the long table in the paneled dining room. Professor Collins sat at the head of the table; Hampstead was on his left and Irma on his right. All during the meal, Irma had been fascinated by the lawyer's weird looks and manner. Now he revealed a toothy smile and said, "Perhaps the most macabre legend associated with this old house concerns the first Barnabas Collins."

"Really?" Irma felt that the lawyer was trying to use his stories to frighten her into leaving Collinwood.

He nodded. "Yes. A wild, dark-haired beauty from the West Indies came to Collinsport and fell in love with him. But it happened that he was already in love with another girl, Josette."

"And a jealous rivalry between the girls followed?"

"Angelique became extremely jealous. When she knew she could not have Barnabas for herself she contrived to have him bitten by a bat which passed on the vampire curse to him."

Professor Collins listened with interest. "The vampire legend is an ancient one."

"From that moment on," Hampstead said solemnly, "Barnabas Collins became one of the living dead. His whole way of life was changed. He was never seen during the hours of daylight.

But when darkness came he would roam the estate and the streets of Collinsport like a lost soul."

"Was there any proof beyond his change of habits that he'd become a vampire?" Irma wanted to know.

"Proof in plenty," the lawyer said, as the candlelight made his odd features stand out from the shadows. "Not long after that, young women of the village began being attacked by some phantom creature. Odd bite marks showed on their throats. They were always found wandering in a dazed condition or unconscious. It took little imagination on the part of the local people to decide that Barnabas had attacked these young women in his desperate thirst for blood."

"Weren't they assuming a lot?" she asked. "Surely these young women could have been attacked by someone else?"

"It was decided that Barnabas Collins was the guilty one. He was ordered from Collinsport. Even his family turned their backs on him. He was a debauched creature who slept in a coffin by day and feasted on the blood of their womenfolk in the dark hours."

"He then moved to London?" Irma's father suggested.

"Somewhere in England," the lawyer said. "He established the British branch of the family over there. And through the years his sons and grandsons have visited here."

"They have access to the old house, don't they?" she said.

"Yes," the lawyer agreed. "That dates back to the will made by a relative of the original Barnabas. The descendants have been less open to criticism, but their behavior has not always been beyond reproach."

Gerald asked, "Have you met the present Barnabas?"

"Yes," Hampstead sneered. "He has been here several times."

"What is he like?" her father wanted to know.

The lawyer placed the tips of his fingers on the edge of the table and hesitated a moment before replying. "On his last stay in the area several girls were attacked in the manner attributed to his ancestor. It was rumored that he suffered from the same curse."

Irma frowned. "But surely that is nonsense!"

"I'm only repeating what the villagers have said."

She asked, "Did he keep the same kind of hours? Restrict his appearances to the night as the original Barnabas did?"

"I believe so," the lawyer said. "I cannot be sure."

"Did he offer an explanation for what happened?" Collins queried.

"When he was spoken to about the attacks he pretended to know nothing of them. A few days later he vanished with his mute servant, Hare, who always accompanies him."

Irma stared at the lawyer. "Would the villagers protest if Barnabas should return?"

"Only if there were more attacks," he said. "Otherwise they have short memories. It is one of the things such criminals count on."

"But he is not a criminal!" she protested, defending the man she'd never seen.

Hampstead smiled grimly. "Isn't that a matter of opinion?"

"At least it has never been proved that he is guilty of any criminal offense," Gerald Collins interjected swiftly. "And now I suggest we adjourn to the living room." Hampstead did not remain long after that. Having managed to get his free meal, he seemed restless to be on his way. He left after thanking them and assuring them of his eagerness to be of assistance in any problems they might have.

When they were alone again Irma asked her father, "What did you make of Mr. Hampstead?"

He sighed. "A most unusual fellow."

They were standing in the shadowed reception hall and she gave him a meaningful look. "I'd say he was very anxious to get us out of here. All those ghost stories were meant to work on my nerves."

"I thought that was fairly obvious."

Irma shuddered. "And the ironical part of it is that I believe there are worse terrors here that he isn't even aware of."

"Don't allow that imagination to work overtime," her father warned.

"I mean it," she said.

"Hampstead is a shrewd character. I don't think we should depend on him too much."

"I'm sure we shouldn't. And that associate of his, Captain Westhaven, struck me as being an old villain."

Gerald nodded. "I noticed that he didn't dwell much on the captain or his past career. He wanted to skim over it."

"For some very good reason," she said.

"Well, at least we are aware of Hampstead's veiled hostility and we can be on the lookout for any tricks he may want to play on us. That should offer us some protection."

"But will it be enough?"

"I hope so," he said. "I did all I could to let him understand we have no thought of selling the estate."

"He'll not give up that easily," Irma predicted.

"I dare say he won't," her father said. "But I'll not change my mind."

He returned to the library to work and she mounted the stairway to the second floor where her room was located. When she reached the landing she came face to face with Juan, who was on his way down.

She had not paid too much attention to him until the long voyage when she had come to know him better. He was dark-skinned, with a thin, bent body and white hair. She asked, "What have you been doing?"

"On the roof," he said, avoiding her eyes.

"Looking after the livestock?"

"Yes," he said.

Something furtive in his manner bothered her. She said, "What does my father have up there?"

Juan looked down. His white servant's coat did not fit well and hung from his shoulders. He made no reply. Irma could see that he didn't want to talk to her about it, but she was concerned so she persisted. "Go on. Please tell me."

He glanced up at her. "Creatures of the air."

"Birds?"

"Yes, miss."

"What sort of birds?"

"Many kind. You better ask Professor," Juan said and at once escaped from her questioning to glide down the stairs.

Irma's pretty face was shadowed. His answers hadn't satisfied her and she had an urge to go up and look for herself but she remembered it was dark and it would be foolhardy to try opening the crates alone. Better to be patient and wait.

Irma undressed for bed filled with forebodings about the future at Collinwood. Then she went to the window to stare out at the ocean. Everything seemed very quiet on the grounds. After a few minutes she snuffed out the candle and slid between the cool bedsheets. She had no idea how long she lay there before she heard the weird bump against her window, which sounded as if some bird had accidentally come up against it in flight.

Sitting up, she listened again. A moment later the bumping was repeated. She was almost sure the glass would be broken but it wasn't. Then there was only silence. But the silence itself was frightening. Irma lay back against the pillow and tried to think what the bumping might have been. The roar of the ocean in the background suggested sea gulls to her and she attempted to calm her fears with the thought that it had been stray gulls which had hit her window.

This upsetting experience was forgotten in the busy hours of the following day. Mrs. Branch took her on a tour of the house and she was astounded by the number of rooms and the variety of furniture in them. The housekeeper explained that the furnishings had been added over the years by various members of the family representing many generations.

Some of the rooms were not in use and had not been used

for years. In these dust and cobwebs had collected, but Mrs. Branch explained, "We have all we can do to keep the parts that are lived in clean and tidy."

"I'm sure of that," she agreed.

In one of the rooms not generally used Irma found a pencil likeness of Quentin Collins in a dust-covered silver frame. She recognized him at once. The housekeeper noticed that she was staring at the drawing.

Picking the likeness up, Mrs. Branch blew the dust from it. "That's Quentin Collins," she said.

"Yes," Irma nodded. "I recognized him. For a time he was with my father on our expedition in Mexico."

The housekeeper raised her eyebrows. "So that is where he went?"

"He was with us several months."

Mrs. Branch gave her an odd look. "Did you like him, miss?"

Irma paused before answering. "Well, he could be charming when he wished."

"No doubt of that."

"But he was moody and a troublemaker," she went on and with a slight blush, added, "He took too much interest in me. And I didn't like him in that way."

The housekeeper said, "I can well understand that, miss. He always fancied himself one with the ladies."

"He was angry when my father dismissed him from the expedition. It was too bad it had to end in a quarrel."

"Trust Mr. Quentin to see to that," Mrs. Branch said. "He caused more than his share of trouble here."

"From what I've been told I doubt if he'll ever come back again," she said.

Anxiety showed on the housekeeper's face. "We can only pray that he don't, miss. Your father and you don't need that problem."

"I agree," she said, taking the drawing in her own hands for a moment.

"And yet he is quite handsome."

"No one can dispute that."

Irma sighed. "If he behaved just a little better. But then, it may not be his fault. He may not be able to control his disposition."

Mrs. Branch nodded. "Not if what they tell is true."

"What is that?"

"Some say he had evil words spoken against him and when the full of the moon comes he can't control the Devil within him." There was a note of awe in the woman's softly spoken words.

Irma listened, glancing once more at the handsome face in the drawing, then put it back on the table. She said, "Perhaps we should not try to judge him."

"Yes, miss," the older woman agreed quietly and they moved on to the attic area. Finally she paused by a door that led to a short flight of stairs. "Up there is the roof and the Captain's Walk."

Irma was at once curious. "I'd like to go up there. My father has some of his live specimens in crates in the Captain's Walk."

"Yes, Juan makes continual trips up to the roof," Mrs. Branch said. "Does your father have some valuable creatures in those crates?"

"I can't tell you," she said. "But I would like to go up there."

Mrs. Branch led the way up the short, steep stairway and they came out in the elevated tower known as the Captain's Walk. The crates were set out at one side of it, ominous in appearance with the dark air holes showing at intervals. Irma went over and tapped the side of one of them, then listened intently.

"Is there anything stirring in there, miss?" the housekeeper asked.

"Not that I can tell," Irma said, still listening.

"Perhaps Juan took whatever was in the case out," she said.

"Perhaps." Irma straightened up and walked away from the crates. "I guess we shouldn't interfere with them. They are not our business."

"True, miss."

She was worried about them just the same but didn't want the housekeeper to realize it so she pretended to be interested in the view from this high point which was surely impressive. "You can see for miles!"

"It is a wonderful spot to see the countryside," Mrs. Branch said.

"The village doesn't look as far distant as it is."

"No, miss."

She glanced down at the grounds, a dizzying distance below. "The stables and the outbuildings look like little huts from up here."

"I know," Mrs. Branch said. "Some of those working in the stables say Professor Collins has many real monster creatures in the cages out there. Animals the like of which they never saw before."

"He has collected some scarce specimens," she agreed.

"One of the maids says that Juan told her to keep away from the crates in the cellar because they have snakes in them."

Irma glanced at the woman and saw that she looked worried. "He does have a collection of snakes," she agreed. "Some of them are poisonous, but many of them are harmless. There's no danger as long as they don't get out of the crates."

"I tried to tell the girl that," Mrs. Branch said, "but she was some afraid. I finally quieted her by telling her she needn't go down to the cellar again."

"That was wise. Let her get over her fear first."

"It's all new to them," Mrs. Branch apologized. "I guess you and the professor are used to having such creatures around."

"I've never felt happy about it," she said in grim understatement. "Now I guess we should go downstairs. Father will be wondering what has become of me."

When she reached the ground floor she came upon her father and Juan in one of the hallways. They were having an excited conversation in Juan's native tongue. Professor Collins spoke it fluently but Irma couldn't understand it. When she joined them the conversation ended and Juan left in the same furtive fashion that had caused her to worry before.

Staring after him, she said, "What is wrong with him?"

"One of the animals in the stable died," her father said. "It's very annoying since we've been here only a short time."

"What happened to it?"

"I don't know," he said. "It could be one of many things. These jungle animals don't take easily to being confined."

"You shouldn't have brought any of them back," she told him.

"I have no intention of defending my position on that again," he said impatiently.

So the talk between them ended. They had lunch and then went for a stroll about the grounds of the estate. She took him as far as the original home of the Collins family.

Gerald Collins stared at its drawn shutters. "I'd call that really desolate-looking."

"I imagine when Barnabas Collins arrives he opens the shutters," she said. "Then it would look much different."

"It would have to," Gerald observed dryly.

They walked past the ancient house to the rise of grassy hill over which the weird trespasser of the day before had vanished. Standing there together in the blazing afternoon sun, they could make out the cemetery at the bottom of the field and the forest of evergreens beyond it.

Her father's face took on an interested expression. "I think I know that cemetery. I have memories of it from my childhood. It is the Collins family burial place."

"Now it will be our responsibility," she said. "I suppose we should go down and investigate the condition it is in."

"I would expect it to be well-cared-for," Collins said. "All our ancestors found their final resting place down there."

She glanced at him. "All but the original Barnabas Collins, who went to England."

"Yes," he agreed. "There is that exception. We may as well pay a short visit to the place."

The grass was high in the field and the surface of the ground uneven. Her long skirt trailed in the grass and she had difficulty walking in her tight formal shoes. Her father had no such problems and marched ahead. At last they reached the stone gates of the cemetery and went inside.

The first tombstone they looked at bore the name of "Josiah Collins" along with his birth and death dates. "He was one of the first of our line to live here," her father said.

It was hot and Irma began to regret she had suggested visiting the cemetery. It was in excellent condition as her father had predicted. The gravestones were in good shape and the grass cut. It had been carefully weeded and the paths were not overgrown. In the hot sunlight a quiet had settled over the cemetery. Not even an insect seemed in evidence, nor were there any birds around. It was as if nature had taken a pause on this blazing day.

"There are some tombs over here," her father said, leading her to the rear of the cemetery where a few trees stood, their branches affording scant shade.

She joined him before a tomb of white granite. A rusty door marked its entrance and several stone steps led down to it. She said, "I gather these are used for entire families."

"Exactly," Professor Collins agreed. "Rather than having separate burial lots, the coffins are placed in one giant underground room."

"It seems to have been popular," she said. "There are several such tombs here."

"The ground could not have been hard to excavate," her father said.

Irma's eyes had been fixed on the rusty iron door of the tomb and as she watched she was sure she saw it move just a trifle. For a moment she felt that it must have been the heat waves which had created the illusion. But as she continued to stare at the rusty door it moved again. She grasped her father's arm. "Look! The door!"

He gazed at her in surprise, then looked at the door and gasped!

The door was certainly moving. Slowly it scraped outward to reveal the darkness of the tomb beyond and then a weird face peered out at them from the shadows.

"Captain Westhaven!" Irma cried when she recognized the old man who was slowly emerging from the dark underground place.

"Yes, I'm Westhaven," he said in his rasping voice as he paused at the foot of the stone steps to lean on his knobby walking stick.

"You don't remember me?" she said.

His surly lower lip was thrust out aggressively. "No!"

"You met me yesterday in front of the old house!" Captain Westhaven glowered at her from under his bushy white eyebrows. Then he proceeded to climb up the stone steps, groaning a little as he did. When he reached the top he stared at her closely.

"Aye," he exclaimed. "Now I know you. You're the daughter of the new owner."

"And I am the new owner," her father said, stepping forward angrily to face the captain. "May I ask what you were doing trespassing in that tomb?"

The stubborn, lined face showed no particular expression, and the sullen eyes were unblinking. "You're Professor Gerald Collins?"

"Yes," he answered angrily.

"The line grows weaker," Captain Westhaven said with disgust.

Irma had never seen her father in such a rage. His face became purple.

"I have not asked for your opinion regarding my family line," he snapped. "I want to know why you are on my property, and more particularly, why you are in this cemetery? And what you were doing in that tomb?"

The old man leaned on his walking stick and smiled tormentingly. "Shade," he said.

"What?" Gerald Collins demanded.

"Shade," Captain Westhaven repeated calmly.

"Shade?" the professor exclaimed. "Are you giving that as a reason for desecrating that tomb?"

"Coolest place I've been able to find. At my age the heat is hard to take."

"There must be plenty of places on your own property where you could be cool," her father challenged. "Don't tell me you had to come over here."

"No cemetery at my place, no tombs. That tomb is like a cold cellar. It even has a bench. I sit down there for hours at a time."

Irma was astonished at his ghoul-like behavior. "Don't you feel strange down in that place of the dead?"

He grinned sourly. "I'm a lot closer to them than I am to you. Got my own casket all finished and waiting for me in my cellar."

Gerald Collins was still looking angry. "There is no excuse for your conduct, sir. I will refrain from speaking my full mind because of your age and the presence of my daughter. But I warn you, I don't want to find you here again."

Captain Westhaven looked unimpressed. "You made a mistake coming here. It's bound to be bad for you. You should have taken our offer for the place."

"I have my own opinions about that as well," Mr. Collins said angrily.

Westhaven nodded. "I can tell you have a lot to learn yet, young fella."

"I'll surely not learn them from you," Irma's father said, outraged. He marched down the steps of the tomb to draw the creaking door shut. "And I'll order you off my property!"

"Maybe you better be careful what you're letting loose on and over other people's property!"

Professor Collins stopped short and stared at the captain. "What do you mean?"

"I guess you know right enough," Captain Westhaven said with a crooked smile that revealed a few yellow teeth.

"I say you're talking nonsense!"

"And I say there was something monstrous that flew over my place at midnight last night and killed one of my lambs!"

Her father had gone white. He stared at the old man with a look that was close to fear. "What are you trying to say?"

"I guess you know. The throat of that lamb was tore wide open. It didn't have a chance."

"I had nothing to do with that," Gerald Collins said.

"Maybe not," Captain Westhaven said with a vengeful smile. "But I think I can make my charge stick. A lot of people know you've brought a cargo of monsters here and they've been talking about what a menace they would be if they got loose so you better not say too much, young man."

"I am no young man," the professor raged, "and I have met people like you in my life before. Your idle threats don't jar me at all."

"Better listen to me," he jeered.

"Come along, Irma," her father said. "I don't want to hear anymore of this."

"You won't get far with your monsters around here! You'll be begging us to buy you out!" Westhaven threatened.

They had gone a few steps and her father turned a moment to answer him.

"Don't worry about buying me out. I have no intention of leaving!"

"With that flying snake loose you may not have a choice. The people here could make you leave!" Captain Westhaven snarled.

Irma was shocked by the old man's words and further shocked by the look of despair that had suddenly crossed her father's face. All the fight seemed to suddenly have wilted out of him.

He stared at the Captain blankly. "You're a wicked old man," he declared in a tight voice.

The ancient guffawed. "I thought you would come around to listening. Just as you'll come around to deciding to sell!"

Gerald Collins turned away from the old man and, taking Irma's arm again, said in a low voice, "Let's get out of here!"

She felt ill. "Aren't you going to force him to leave the cemetery?"

Her father kept on walking. "He'll leave."

"I wouldn't let him have it all his own way if I were in your place," she complained.

His head was bent. "It doesn't matter."

She said no more until they were out of the cemetery and on their way up through the field. Then she drew on her parent's arm and forced him to come to a halt while she turned and looked back in the direction of the burial place.

"He hasn't left yet," she said.

"I don't care," Professor Collins said dejectedly.

Irma gazed at him with wide eyes. "You're afraid of him!"

"No!"

"I'm sure you are!"

"Why should I be?"

"Because he knows something," she declared. "Something you've been keeping from me."

Her father's face was white. "What are you saying?"

"Now I know what you and Juan were talking about. Why you were both so upset?"

He stared at her with seeming fear. "Don't talk nonsense!"

"It's not nonsense," she declared. "No animal died as you pretended, but that monstrous thing you had in the crate up in the Captain's Walk has somehow escaped! The feathered serpent is free to terrorize us all!"

CHAPTER 6

Her words had a shattering effect on her father. He stood there in silence for a moment, unable to decide how to answer her. His agitated state along with the way he had behaved when confronted by the strange old man led Irma to believe that her worst fears were justified.

"Answer me!" she cried.

He made a weak gesture. "What can I say? All this is a product of your imagination!"

"No!" she protested. "I saw the way you acted in the cemetery and your reaction now."

"Because I simply can't believe you'd take that man's charge seriously," her father said brokenly. "I can't see you taking his word against mine."

"I've suspected it all along. There were rumors on the ship. And last night some strange thing bumped against my window. I was terrified!"

Professor Collins licked his lips nervously. "I don't know what it was that hit your windows but it was no feathered serpent. There is no such creature except in Aztec legends."

"Legends are based on facts. There had to be something to start the worship of a feathered serpent god!"

"I won't go into that," he said wearily. "I can only tell you I brought no such monster back with me."

Her eyes met his. "You lied to me about the Dimetrodon and we were both nearly killed by it."

"That was different!"

"I think not," she said. "You have this strange dedication to science that goes beyond truth."

"Irma!" he reproached her.

"You have lied to me before in the name of science and research. You'll do it again," she said firmly. "You're probably conspiring with Juan to try to get that monster recaptured in some way!"

"That's not so!"

She studied him sadly. "I wish I could believe you, Father. But I can't. Not after all that has happened."

He looked back in the direction of the cemetery. "That man is mad. It is plain enough. How can you accept his word against mine?"

"He defied you and he's still there trespassing."

"That's of no importance," he said.

"I say it is," she told him, "and I think he and Hampstead are out to bring you to your knees."

"If that is so, why are you turning against me too? I need your support."

"Because I'm afraid of what you may have done," she said.

"How can I convince you I'm telling the truth?" he demanded.

"There's no way," she said unhappily. "We'll just have to wait and see what takes place next."

Without giving him a chance to reply, Irma resumed the uphill walk to Collinwood. All during the journey back there was an awkward silence between them. She did not want to quarrel with her father, for she knew that whatever he had done had been in what he believed the best interests of his profession. Yet she could not forgive him if he had recklessly placed countless lives in danger, including their own.

If he had placed the residents of Collinwood and the village in jeopardy he had reason to be afraid. If the people became convinced he had unleashed a monster to prey on them they would reject him. He would not be able to continue living in the family mansion. He would have no choice but to sell the property. And that, of course, was what Hampstead and Captain Westhaven wanted.

The tragic thing was that he had played so completely into their hands. Irma tried to force herself to believe that there was perhaps a bare chance that her father was telling her the truth, but in view of the shipboard rumors and all the rest she doubted it. Because she had not yet seen the feathered serpent nor heard testimony to its existence from anyone else she could depend on, she could cling to a single, slender hope.

Even if there should be no feathered serpent, there were all those other creatures he'd brought back along with the crates of treasure. Mrs. Branch had already mentioned that the stable men were awed by the things in the cages left out there, and one of the maids had been on the verge of hysteria because of discovering the snakes in the cellar. This murmuring would build. There was almost bound to be some incident and then the anger of the help and the villagers would be turned against her father.

The pleasant dreams she'd had before reaching Collinwood were now rudely shattered. She was not much more at ease on this great estate than she had been in the jungle. Her father had brought all the problems which had plagued her there along with him. Now she had nothing to look forward to but the almost bleak certainty that he'd be forced to let the estate go to the two who wanted it for a pittance.

When she reached Collinwood she went directly to her room. She slept until before dinner. When she went downstairs she was pleasantly surprised to find her father having sherry with a welcome visitor—Stuart Jennings.

Smiling, she went over to him. "It's good to see you."

"And to see you again," he said. "Your father tells me you have worked hard adjusting to this new setting."

"We're all unpacked now," she said.

Her father brought her a sherry and he looked much relieved. "It took this young man to make you smile," he said and then added, "we must have you here often."

Stuart smiled. "That's something I'll look forward to."

Professor Collins was in a happy mood. "What we should have here is a fine ball. Some good music, fine food, and a night of dancing until the small hours."

Irma was forced to smile at her father's statement. "I've never known you to have such social aspirations before. You have always seemed most happy in some remote jungle."

"You do not know what I was like in my youth," he said. "Before your mother died we lived a full social life. I was considered something of a prize waltzer. It is time I harked back to those days again. And what more excuse do I need than a beautiful daughter like you?"

"Hear! Hear!" Stuart laughed, raising his sherry glass.

Irma couldn't help but be caught up in the bright mood of the others. For a moment it all seemed possible. "Such an affair needs planning, plenty of help and a suitable room."

Her father waved a hand around to indicate the double living rooms. "I doubt if you'll find a better setting for a ball anywhere in the county than in these rooms. Isn't that so, young man?"

"I must agree with your father," Stuart told her. "The benefits of such an evening could be untold. It would at once introduce you to all the important people in the area, the people you need to have as friends if you are to succeed here."

"You see," Professor Collins said.

Irma sighed. "It is something to think about. I wouldn't want to attempt it until things are more stable with us."

"But that could be the way to make them more stable," her father enthused. "Try and coax her into it, Jennings."

All during dinner her father made references to the proposed ball. When he wasn't talking about that, he was answering Stuart's questions about the many expeditions he'd headed and the research he'd instigated. Irma sat quietly and listened to them. After they left the dining room her father excused himself and went to the study to work. For the first time she was left alone with Stuart.

"Shall we go for a stroll?" he asked. "It's at least a half-hour until dusk."

"I'd like that," she agreed, anxious to get out of the house for a while. She found a lace shawl to throw over her shoulders in case it should be chilly and joined Stuart on the front steps.

"We'll go as far as Widows' Hill," he said. "There's a bench there. If you don't find it too cool we can sit and talk."

She gave a relieved sigh. "You can have no idea how much that appeals to me. I haven't the same feelings about this house that Father has."

Stuart looked serious as he escorted her down the steps. "I know you had some misgivings about it when you first arrived. I hoped you might get over them."

"I'm afraid they have instead increased."

"Why?"

"Things have been happening. Lawyer Hampstead came here and I don't like him at all," Irma confessed.

"He's the one who has been creating the troubles about the boundary between the woodlands belonging to Collinwood and my father's lumber land," Stuart said with a frown.

"It seems he's trying to get this property for himself and that awful Captain Westhaven."

"They are both unscrupulous men," he worried.

"And I'm afraid Father has played into their hands."

"In what way?" Stuart questioned.

She hesitated. "I hardly know how to tell you. It's quite fantastic."

"Go on," he said.

They were nearing the path that ran along the cliff and she searched her mind for some way to begin. Finally she said, "Since we've arrived, have you heard any unpleasant rumors?"

"Such as?"

"About my father's work."

He looked slightly uneasy. "There was some gossip at the dock but I don't think any attention should be paid to it."

She gave him a keen side glance. "Tell me about it."

"If you like," he said, "but I still consider it nonsense."

"I must hear."

"Some of the workers there spread a story that one of the crates of livestock contained a horrible monster—a large snake with wings!"

"I knew it," she gasped.

"What?"

"Lawyer Hampstead has already spread his malicious gossip to try and turn the local people against us."

"What does it matter since it's only gossip?" Stuart said lightly.

"That's the trouble," Irma said quietly. "It may be true."

This came as such a surprise for him that he halted and turned to face her. "What did you say?"

"There could be truth in the rumor," she said unhappily. "I can't be certain. My father denies that he ever brought back such a creature but he has held back the truth from me before."

"You must be joking," Stuart said incredulously.

"I wish I were," she said and went on to tell him all that she knew.

By the time she'd finished her account they'd reached Widows' Hill. Stuart had listened to all she had to say with an expression of great concern. Now he stood on the high cliff staring down at the waves as they dashed in on the rocky shore below.

He said, "But you could be wrong. Your father may be telling the truth. There doesn't have to be any feathered serpent."

"I know that," she agreed. "But there is strong evidence that there could be. Don't forget that awful Captain Westhaven said some monster swooped down on his herd of sheep and ripped the throat of one open."

"He is capable of telling any lie."

"There was that strange bumping against my window in the night."

He frowned. "It could have been a bat or a bird."

"I try to tell myself that."

He gave her a sympathetic look. "You mustn't let your nerves take over. You have to fight this."

Irma sat on the wooden bench and drew her shawl about her shoulders. The daylight was beginning to fade and from the distance she could see the first rotating beam of a distant lighthouse.

She said, "Father says I mustn't give in to my fears."

"That's so," he agreed, sitting by her. "Whether he is telling the truth or not."

"The tragedy is that whether there is such a monster or not we'll be in just as much trouble if those two men convince the villagers one exists."

"And that's what they'll try to do."

"I'm positive of that."

"There must be some way to defeat them," Stuart said.

"But how?"

He smiled. "Hold a big party as your father suggests?"

"I'd like to," Irma said with sadness in her voice. "But there are some other things that must be settled first."

Stuart took one of her hands in his and earnestly said, "You know I'm on your side, Irma. Whatever I can do, I will do."

"I know that," she said gently.

He went on, "I don't know how my father and your father will get along. There is dispute about the lumber land border. But even if they should quarrel I want us to remain friends."

"Let's trust that nothing like that happens," she said.

"I surely do," he agreed. "From the moment I met you on the schooner I felt you'd play a special part in my life."

She felt her cheeks warm. "How could you feel that?"

"I fell in love with you then," he said simply.

"But you hardly know me," she protested.

"I know you as well as I need to," Stuart assured her quietly and he took her in his arms for a lasting kiss.

Irma offered no resistance, though the young man's sudden embrace had come as a surprise. She liked and trusted him, and thought that perhaps the best thing that had happened to her since arriving at Collinwood was Stuart Jennings.

He gently released her and smiling, said, "There! Now you know how I feel about you. I'd like your permission to ask your father for your hand in marriage as soon as possible."

She studied him with loving eyes. "Not yet, Stuart. Not until some of our other problems are solved. But I do care for you!"

"Let's not wait too long," he pleaded. "I'm worried for you and what might happen here. There is too much tension in the air."

"I can't desert my father."

"I would like to see us married and you away from Collinwood," he said firmly.

Irma glanced back at the lighted windows of the distant

house and gave a tiny shudder. "I still fear Collinwood, but I must go on living there until I'm sure things are going to be all right with Father."

"I won't rest easy until we're married," he said.

"Please, don't let's talk about that anymore at present," she begged him. "We'll have to be patient."

The rest of the evening offered nothing as exciting as those moments. After a short time Stuart saw her back to the front entrance of Collinwood. They enjoyed a final goodnight kiss and she went inside with a feeling of happiness quite new to her. It wasn't surprising that the night that followed was uneventful and her sound sleep was not marred.

Morning brought fog and a drizzle of rain. Irma had not been aware how awful the weather at Collinwood could be until she looked out at the chilly, wet morning. She had breakfast with her father and had a hard time hiding her elation about the previous evening. Her father spoke of Stuart in glowing terms and this pleased her.

It was just as they were finishing breakfast that the start of a strange series of events began. Mrs. Branch came into the dining room, a puzzled look on her broad face, and told the professor, "There's a man at the door to see you. He won't give his name but says he must talk to you himself."

"Is he a villager?" Mr. Collins asked.

"No," the housekeeper said. "I've never set eyes on him before."

"What sort of person is he?"

Mrs. Branch looked uneasy. "It's hard for me to describe him," she said. "But he has an odd, foreign look. I'd say he was a seafaring man."

Gerald nodded. "No doubt someone I've met in my travels. Have him wait. I'll talk to him after I finish breakfast."

"Yes, sir," Mrs. Branch said and left.

Irma was worried. "I hope this doesn't mean more trouble."

"I don't think so," he said. "You can stay and hear what he has to say if you like."

"I want to do that," she agreed.

When they left the dining room they went directly to the living room, where Mrs. Branch had told the caller to wait. The moment they appeared he jumped up eagerly and Irma thought he was one of the strangest-looking persons she had ever encountered. Mrs. Branch had been correct in judging him a seafaring man. He had the authentic air of a sailor. His hair, tousled and long, was iron-gray, and he had a short iron-gray beard to match it. His skin was bronzed and over his left eye there was a large black eye-patch. His single good eye seemed to have no eyebrow.

Across his right cheek there was a deep, livid scar as if it had been sliced open with a knife or a sword.

"Professor Collins?" he inquired in a grating voice as he limped over to meet them.

"Yes," her father said. "And this is my daughter, Irma. Who are you?"

"Jim, Matey," the man rasped. "Jim Davis is my full John Henry. But no one calls me anything but Jim."

The man held out a rough hand and Gerald Collins shook hands with him and said, "You wanted to see me?"

"Right, Matey," the old salt said with a grim smile. "I sure have been waiting to have a talk with you."

"You can speak freely before my daughter."

The sailor glanced at Irma with his shrewd single eye. "You folks are new here."

"Yes, we are," her father said.

"So am I," Jim Davis rasped. "Came in on the night boat from Boston last night. I'm lookin' for a job here and I figured you could use me."

Gerald Collins stared at the sailor. "What makes you think that? We have a full household staff and also outside help."

Jim Davis' single eye was fixed on Professor Collins. "I understand you got some animals you brought back from Mexico."

"Yes, I have," her father said. "But my man, Juan, is taking care of them."

"From what I heard it's too big a job for one man," Jim Davis rasped, "and I'm familiar with all kinds of tropical animals and birds."

The professor rubbed his chin. "I believe Juan can manage alone."

"Better think it over careful," the sailor said. "If any of those critters got free it could cost you some headaches."

"I believe the danger of that is small," her father said.

The sailor looked crafty. "There's talk in town that you shouldn't have brought that livestock back here at all, and that some kind of monster is already loose. I've only been here a few hours and I've heard that."

Irma saw her father's face pale and he said nervously, "Your information is wrong."

"Story began with a character called Captain Westhaven," he continued. "Understand he is a neighbor of yours."

"He is and he's a crazy old man," Collins said.

The sailor chuckled. "Jim Davis knows that better than most. The truth is, Matey, I sailed under Westhaven a dozen years ago."

"You did?" Gerald gasped.

"I did," the sailor repeated slyly. "And if the occasion called for it I could tell a few stories about the kind of cargo that made him rich—stories that would hurt him some around here."

Irma's interest was awakened. She recalled the mention Mrs. Branch had made of Captain Westhaven's criminal past. "What sort of cargo did he deal in?"

The gray-bearded salt shifted from one foot to another and his single good eye held a crafty gleam. "Truth is, it's something that shouldn't be mentioned before the likes of a gentle female like you. But to put it as neat as I can, he dealt in black gold."

"Black gold!" Professor Collins said in a shocked tone. "You're saying that he was a slaver?"

"I sailed the coast of Africa with him for more than three years," the sailor said smugly. "And I know. And I can show proof of what I say."

Irma exchanged a surprised glance with her father. Then she asked the sailor, "What sort of proof?"

"Documents," he said, winking his good eye, "documents I filched from the ship before I deserted which would blacken his character in any court!"

There was a silence in the room. Irma was trying to make up her mind whether or not he was telling the truth. It seemed to her that he was. Mrs. Branch had suggested there were rumors about Westhaven's dark past already being whispered in the village. This merely confirmed it. It seemed to her a stroke of good fortune that Jim Davis should have come to them for work.

Turning to her father, she said, "I think you should hire him. Juan badly needs help."

Professor Collins hesitated. "I don't know."

"I'm a good hand with any kind of animal," said Davis.

"And your testimony as to Captain Westhaven's character or lack of it might be useful in event we have trouble with that crazy old man," Irma told him.

The sailor chuckled. "Nothing would please me better than to tell a court how he abused them poor slaves he carried aboard that stinking schooner."

Gerald Collins sighed. "I believe we can use you, Jim Davis. I'll take you down to the cellars to meet Juan and he'll instruct you in your duties."

"Right, Matey," the sailor said with a grin and nodded to Irma, "You've got a wise head as well as a pretty one on those shoulders of yours, miss."

Irma did not answer him as she watched him limp off after her father. As they vanished down the corridor in search of Juan she felt this might be another turn of good fortune in their favor. It had started with Stuart proposing to her last night. And now, just when everything seemed at its worst, there had turned up this sailor with the evidence to blacken Captain Westhaven's character if he should make further attempts to injure them.

Her father confirmed this viewpoint when he joined her later. "I think that old sailor will work well with Juan," he said. "If the worst comes to the worst we can use him to blackmail Captain Westhaven and Hampstead."

"I was thinking the same thing," she said.

"It could be that our luck has changed," Gerald Collins said.

Irma had no idea then that they were gravely in error – that within a few more hours something would happen to make things look even blacker than they had before.

Irma did not see Stuart that evening and that left her feeling isolated and depressed. She went to bed early but her sleep was restless. Once, long after midnight, she was wakened by a shrill scream from somewhere on the grounds. She sat up in bed and stared into the darkness with her heart pounding but the scream was not repeated again.

She had begun to relax and believed that she might have dreamed the scream when something else happened to alarm her. There came a weird scraping bump on her window and summoning all her courage, Irma quickly got out of bed and ran to the window in her bare feet. She drew back the drapes and stared out to see the first streaking of dawn in the remaining darkness. Then she saw something else that made her hold her breath for a moment! Faraway a weird-looking creature was flying over the bay. It could have been a bird, perhaps a gull, but she thought it had a longer body. Then it vanished against a black cloud.

She left the window with fear shadowing her lovely face and slept only fitfully for the balance of the night. She awoke to another dull day, although the fog had wafted out some to linger over the bay and ocean beyond but leave the land free. The experiences of the night still haunted her. Once again the obsession that Collinwood held unknown horror for her filled her mind.

As she went downstairs she was aware of low, excited voices in the hallway and the front door slammed closed in a startling way. She continued on down to the bottom of the steps with growing apprehension. She saw her father standing there alone, his back to her, unaware of her presence.

Irma called to him, "What is wrong?"

He wheeled around to stare up at her white-faced. "Something dreadful!"

She quickly came down the rest of the stairs. "Tell me!"

His face registered horror. "Last night one of the gardeners was killed."

"No!" She remembered that scream.

"They found him out on the lawn just now." He paused. "His throat was torn open and there was an expression of mad fear on his face!"

Her eyes met her father's. "I was afraid this would happen."

"They've sent word to the village," he went on in a weary voice. "It doesn't look like murder. Probably the work of some wild thing."

"Of course," she said bitterly.

Professor Collins stared at her in alarm. "You're not thinking—" He left his statement unfinished.

"What else can I think?"

"There is no feathered serpent!" he protested.

"I don't care what you call it," she said. "I believe there is some monster loose and that it killed that man! I saw some weird thing in the sky after I heard a scream from the lawn last night!"

"You, of all people, should believe me!"

"I'm sorry, Father," she said. "I'd like to but I can't."

Her father said nothing. He turned and walked off down the shadowed corridor to his study, the slump of his shoulders indicating his great sorrow.

Irma watched him go and sighed deeply. She was debating whether to follow him or not when the knock came on the front door. She tried to collect herself as she went over and opened it.

Standing there was a handsome man whom Irma recognized at once. He wore a caped-coat and carried a black cane with a silver wolf's head. He bowed to her and said, "I'm sorry to disturb you but I felt I should introduce myself and let you know I've come to Collinwood for a short stay."

"You don't have to," Irma said. "I can guess who you are. You're Barnabas Collins."

CHAPTER 7

The gaunt, handsome face of the man showed a melancholy smile. "You are right," he said. "I am Barnabas Collins. How did you know?"

"The portrait here in the hall, for one thing."

He glanced up at the gold-framed portrait. "Of course. I'd forgotten."

"And then I have heard so much about you from others. You fitted the description given me completely," she said. "Please come in."

Barnabas stepped into the shadowed hallway, a striking figure in his caped-coat. His dark brown hair fell in orderly disarray about his forehead and at his temples and his eyes were also brown and deep-set. He had an air of charm and poise which Irma at once sensed.

"And you are Irma Collins," he said. "The daughter of my cousin, Professor Gerald Collins, who has come to take over the estate."

"That is so," she agreed. "How is it you are so familiar with the facts about us?"

"Like yourself, I have been well-informed by third parties," he said. His voice had a mellow ring and there was only a hint of a British accent to it.

She said, "My father has just retired to his study. I'll take you to him in a moment—but first I must warn you that you've arrived at a bad time."

His face became grave. "I understand that. I was coming across the lawn when the body of your gardener was found. A sad business."

"A wretched affair," she sighed. "I don't know what it will mean to us here."

"He must have been attacked by some beast of prey," Barnabas Collins said.

"So it would seem," she said faintly, not ready to take the newcomer into her confidence yet.

"There are few such creatures native to this area," Barnabas said, his deep-set eyes studying her. "We did have a wolf scare a year or two ago but that was settled."

"So I understand," she said, assuming he was referring to Quentin Collins and the werewolf affair.

"It's hard to imagine what could have attacked that poor fellow and ripped his throat in such a savage way."

"Baffling!"

Barnabas Collins had a knowing air. "Have you or your father any theories?"

"No," she said vaguely. "He has sent to the village for the proper authority to come and investigate."

An expression of ironic amusement passed over his face. "I would not look for too much help in that direction. Likely the village constable and Saul Hampstead will come. Lawyer Hampstead sits as judge on the local bench."

"I had no idea," she said, dismayed at the prospect.

"I've learned these facts through bitter experience," Barnabas said. "So be prepared for something less than ideal cooperation from the local authorities."

Her pretty face was marred by her upset. "Who can one turn to?"

"I'm afraid you must learn to rely a great deal on your own judgments and actions," he suggested.

"I can see that now," she said in a troubled voice. "Have you come for a visit?"

"Yes. My man, Hare, is presently unpacking my things at the old house, where I always stay. I was on my way to let you know I'd arrived when I stumbled onto the scene of this macabre mystery."

"Not very pleasant for you."

"Or for you," he said sincerely. "I'm sorry this has happened, Miss Collins."

"I've been troubled ever since I entered this old mansion," she told him. "My first impression was that it would bring me ill luck and I'm still of the same opinion."

Barnabas was sympathetic. "You mustn't let the rather grim atmosphere overwhelm you, Miss Collins. Collinwood has known many good days as well as bad ones. To a degree we make our own destiny."

"You can say that in the face of what happened to that man lying out there in the grass?" she asked with a hint of derision.

"That is something beyond your control," he said. "But that is not true of your feelings."

Her eyes widened. "But my feelings are subject to what happens around me!"

"Well stated, Miss Collins. We cannot change the events outside our own orbit. I'm merely trying to suggest that we can choose our reactions to them."

"Aren't my reactions bound to be fear and terror in the face of something such as has just happened?" she demanded with some annoyance.

"You should also try to interpret the happening."

"I'm afraid I have," she said. "And please don't continually address me as Miss Collins. We are cousins, however distant. Wouldn't it be much more friendly for me to call you Barnabas and you use my first name, Irma?"

He smiled. "Thank you, Irma. I'm glad you brought that point up. I'm anxious to get closer to you, to try to understand your thinking. And I can best do that if we're truly friendly."

She offered a wan smile in return. "I see no reason why we shouldn't be friends, Barnabas."

"Good!"

"Now I'll present you to Father," she said, and showed him down the hallway to the study.

Professor Collins was at first annoyed at being intruded on in the midst of a crisis. But as soon as he knew who Barnabas was he warmed up and even went so far as to ask him for his advice. The British cousin looked rather awkward as he heard this suggestion.

"My advice is bound to have little value," he said. "I'm sure you are intelligent enough to make your own decisions."

Gerald sighed. "I assume my daughter has filled you in on the background to this shocking event."

Irma felt she had to speak up. "Not really, Father. I left that for you to explain."

He frowned. "It's a task I'm not suited to," he told Barnabas.

"Don't fret about it," Barnabas said quietly. "I may know more about this than either you or Irma."

Her father eyed him with surprise. "Please explain yourself, sir," he said with dignity.

Barnabas exchanged his cane from one hand to the other. "I'm aware of the scheme of Lawyer Hampstead and Captain Westhaven to take over this property," he calmly informed them.

"It is a fact that they have such a scheme," Mr. Collins said unhappily.

"Part of their plan is to spread so many dark rumors about you and your doings you'll be forced to sell to them and leave," Barnabas said quietly.

"That is the sickness. What is the cure?" Gerald demanded.

"An interesting question," Barnabas observed. "I spent some time in the village and I have heard some of the rumors, especially about your having brought a collection of monsters back from Mexico with you."

"A few live specimens for study," the professor said unhappily.

"A great many if the accounts are true," Barnabas said. "And they go on to say you are keeping many of them here in the house. Talk of a feathered serpent appeared to dominate their fears."

"You are an educated man," Gerald Collins said wearily. "A man of the world, if I may use a familiar term. You must realize how nonsensical that story is."

Barnabas said, "I'm afraid the killing of your servant will have the identical effect on the rumors of oil being tossed on a blaze."

Mr. Collins looked miserable. "I was sitting here thinking that same thing when you came here."

Irma spoke to her parent. "Barnabas believes the local law authority is controlled by Mr. Hampstead. It is likely he will come out here along with the constable to make an investigation and a finding."

Her father sounded concerned. "Of course the finding will be bound to throw additional suspicion on us!"

"You should be prepared for that possibility," Barnabas advised.

"What to do?" The professor spread his hands in despair.

"As a member of the family I am on your side in this," Barnabas said.

"Thank you," Mr. Collins replied.

"I would advise that you be perfectly honest and sure of

your facts," Barnabas told him.

Professor Collins paced back and forth unhappily. "There is nothing I can say. There should be no danger from any of the specimens I have here. My personal servant, Juan, is trained in their care and is most trustworthy. All the precautions one could expect have been observed."

"I see," Barnabas said. "In that case we can only wait and see what the constable and Hampstead have to say."

Gerald nodded. "I expect they'll be here shortly."

"In all likelihood," Barnabas said. "In the meanwhile don't panic."

"Thank you. I'm glad you've made yourself known to us and also made clear your stand. We'll look forward to seeing you often."

Irma and Barnabas left her father in the study and went back to the hallway. At Barnabas' suggestion she got her cloak and they strolled outside. From the steps she could see the small forlorn group standing by the body of the unfortunate gardener, waiting for the village constable to arrive.

Barnabas took her gently by the arm. "There is no need for us to go over there."

"No," she said in a taut voice. The sky was gray with clouds and the day seemed cool and unpleasant.

"We'll stroll towards my place," he suggested.

When they were near the stables she saw Juan and the sailor, Jim, whom her father had engaged the day before, standing in the doorway of the building talking together. "That is Juan," she told the man at her side.

Barnabas halted for a moment and stared at the swarthy, white-haired Juan. "And who is the other one?"

"A sailor," she said. "My father hired him only yesterday."

Barnabas gave her a questioning glance. "Were you in need of extra help?"

"Not really," she said. "But this man claims he is an expert in handling animals. And there was another reason for hiring him. Years ago he sailed under Captain Westhaven and he knows a few interesting facts about him."

Barnabas' gaunt, intelligent face reflected his interest in this news. "Really?"

"Yes."

"Westhaven is an old scoundrel."

"I agree."

"Any tale that fellow might have to tell would not be a pretty one," the Britisher said dryly.

"My father felt his testimony might be helpful if we needed

to marshall evidence against Hampstead and Captain Westhaven."

"An interesting possibility."

"We both thought so."

They moved on by the stables and soon the red brick building known as the old house came into view. She approached it with Barnabas, feeling glad that this seemingly astute man was there to help them.

She suddenly remembered some of the stories she'd heard about him and looking up at him, she said, "I have heard that you rarely if ever appeared in the daylight hours. Yet it is late morning and you have already shown yourself."

Barnabas smiled grimly. "It is true that on some of my previous visits I was only able to appear after dusk settled." He gave her a strange side glance. "You see, I was suffering from an unusual illness which meant that exposure to daylight would be fatal."

She gave a small utterance of surprise. "How awful for you!"

"It was."

"And restricting."

"I found it irksome, indeed," he agreed as they continued to approach the old house, "but now I'm happily freed of that shadow and able to live a normal life again."

"I think that is wonderful," she said. "Are you really cured of your illness?"

A frown creased his brow. "I hope the cure will be permanent," he said. "But there will have to be a period of trial—perhaps several years. If I have no other recurrence then I can call myself safe."

She smiled up at him. "I'm sure you will be. I hope that is how it turns out."

"Thank you, Irma," he said warmly. "Your good wishes give me courage."

She sighed. "I'm positive you're not short on courage. I only wish I had more. My father also could do with some extra."

"But he must be a brave man," Barnabas told her. "He has braved the jungle many times on his expeditions, and you have gone with him."

"I'm thinking of courage of a different sort," she said. They were at the entrance of the old house and she saw that the shutters were still closed. The place had not lost its air of being deserted, yet she knew that Barnabas had already moved in and his servant must be inside.

"Would you like to take a quick look at the inside of the house?" he asked.

She hesitated. "Have I time? I want to be on hand when the constable arrives."

"You should have plenty of time," he assured her. "The Collinsport constable is almost impossible to locate, and then he moves like a snail."

Irma smiled grimly. "Your description continues to disillusion me about the help we'll get from that source."

"I know something about it. I have been exposed to the stupidity and bigotry of the local officials."

"Of course. That's something else I'd forgotten. They spread a lot of gossip about you a few years ago. Didn't they try to make out you had some sort of curse like your ancestor?"

He nodded. "They were kind enough to dub me a vampire."

"That's what I heard!" Irma exclaimed.

"There was a wave of local hysteria," Barnabas said. "I decided that I had better leave here quickly. And I did."

"Of course the hysteria passed."

"It always does," Barnabas said with a twinkle in his deep-set eyes. "I'm positive that if the witches of Salem could have managed to go off for a short holiday their accusers would have lost their enthusiasm and they would never have been burned at the stake. Now we must go inside, since your time is limited."

Irma was glad she'd brought along her cloak. The inside of the old house seemed more chilly than outside. They went down a dark, narrow corridor and then Barnabas ushered her into the living room. It was not as large as the one at Collinwood but was equally decorated and furnished just as beautifully.

Barnabas touched a match to candles on the center table so that they might be able to view the room better. "The heavy drapes let in scant light even with the shutters open," he explained.

"You will be opening them, won't you?" she asked.

"I will, this time," he agreed. "On my other visits because of the odd nature of my illness I preferred to keep the place in near darkness. Of course dampness has been a problem."

"Naturally," she said. "This house is occupied so infrequently."

He sighed. "I have a warm affection for it. I would hate to see it torn down or completely deserted, which would happen if I did not exercise my rights to it."

"Father isn't actually clear about those rights," she said. "Mr. Hampstead didn't explain them properly."

"Then I must discuss the situation with him," Barnabas said pleasantly. "It really isn't complicated."

He picked up one of the candles and led her over to a portrait that hung above the fireplace. "Do you find that girl in the painting attractive?" he asked.

Irma stared at the young, wistful face gazing down at her from the dark canvas. "She's lovely! It's a fine painting—it almost looks as if it had been done by the same artist who painted your ancestor."

Barnabas gave her a look of surprised admiration. "You were quick to note that," he said. "It is the work of the same artist. This is a painting of Josette duPres. There was a romance between her and the first Barnabas Collins."

"She has a sad face."

"The romance ended badly," he said. "She killed herself."

"I'm sorry!" she said.

Barnabas held the flickering candle high to illuminate the painting. It cast a revealing glow on his own sad, handsome face. "She was very young to die that way," he murmured.

"How?"

"You've heard of Widows' Hill?"

"I've been there."

"She threw herself from that high point to the rocks," he said in a weary voice.

"I've heard that tragedies had occurred there," she said. "And so that was one of them."

"Probably the first one."

"It's just as I told you," she said emotionally. "I do not think Collinwood is a happy place. Too much has happened here."

He turned from the painting and lowered the candle a little. "Don't you think the curse on it could be broken?"

"I don't know. I don't really care!"

His eyes met hers. "Shouldn't you care? You are a Collins."

"I don't feel like one. I don't have any love for this place at all."

"That may gradually come to you," he said.

Her eyes were full of fear. "I haven't been honest with you! I know that there's nothing but tragedy and horror ahead for Father and me here. Our only hope is to get away."

"You're trembling!" Barnabas said, touching her arm.

Irma looked away, her eyes moist with tears. "I'm sorry. I didn't intend to make a scene."

"There is no harm done," he said quietly as he replaced the candle on the table. "I wish you would be honest with me."

Irma looked up at his sympathetic face. "Why should we burden you with our troubles?"

"I would like you to consider me your friend," he said.

Impulsively she told him, "I believe my father may not be telling the truth—that he may have brought back some monstrous creature with him."

Barnabas studied her gravely. "You're saying that there may be a feathered serpent?"

"Yes."

"What do you base your belief on?"

"Father has been strange in his denials. He had another weird creature on the schooner, but it was lost at sea. At the time he denied its existence until it got free of its cage and almost killed us."

"I see," Barnabas said.

"He and Juan have also had a lot of harried consultations."

"That could be expected," Barnabas said. "There must be many problems in handling all those live specimens your father brought back from Mexico."

"Father insisted that several of the crates be taken to the rooftop at Collinwood. When I questioned him about this he claimed they were birds and other specimens that would be better up there."

Barnabas was listening attentively. "You think one of those crates may have contained this weird serpent?"

"Yes. I believe it may have escaped somehow. Last night I heard a scream, which must have come from that poor man who was killed. When I went to the window I saw a terrifying silhouette of something flying off towards the ocean."

"You're sure your imagination wasn't playing a trick on you?"

"No."

"So it is your feeling that Hampstead may have a solid case against your father. That because of him there may be a monster at large in the area."

"I don't know what to think," Irma said unhappily.

"In your position it would seem best that you place your trust in your father," Barnabas told her. "It may be that your faith will be betrayed but until you're certain, you owe your loyalty to your father."

"Of course you're right," she agreed. "This way I'm tormenting myself to no purpose."

"Exactly. Time enough to cope with the possible terrors of a flying serpent when you are positive one exists," he said. "Now we should return to the main house. Surely the constable and Hampstead have arrived."

They left the old house without her having seen Barnabas' servant, Hare, though he had mentioned him. She assumed that the servant must have been out somewhere getting provisions or on some other errands.

Walking back briskly, she told Barnabas, "My father and I visited the family cemetery the other day."

"Did you find it interesting?"

"As much as I was able to see of it," she said ruefully. "We'd only barely gotten there when that dreadful old Captain Westhaven came out of one of the tombs and gave me a terrible fright."

"He came out of a tomb?" Barnabas said in surprise.

"Yes. He was very brazen about it. He claimed he went in there regularly on hot days because it offered him a shady retreat."

"It would do that all right. I'd still consider it a strange place for a living person to seek out."

"I agree," she said. "Could there be another reason for his being down there?"

"I'm thinking just that," Barnabas said. "There was a story that one of our ancestors came upon a portion of a lost pirate treasure in an isolated cove along the shore. There was said to be a fortune in precious stones in an ancient chest found at low tide. He was a miserly type and when he knew he was dying he had a special casket constructed with a secret compartment in which he hid the jewels so that when he was buried they went along with him."

"What a strange story," she said.

"From all accounts, Abijah Collins was a strange person. I suspect that our vulture-like Captain Westhaven has heard the tale and has quietly been making a search of the various tombs for the coffin of Abijah."

"It sounds like something he would do," she agreed.

"But the casket wouldn't be all that easy to locate," Barnabas said with bitter humor. "Somewhere along the line several tombs were constructed and the coffins transferred from one to another of them. The records became hopelessly mixed up. Not even the family have any true clues as to what tombs hold which coffins."

"I think that Captain Westhaven would be more interested in the jewels than in finding shade down there," she said. "I must tell father."

Barnabas nodded. "It's likely the old man is wasting his time. It is my personal opinion the whole story is fiction."

"In any case, he shouldn't be trespassing on the estate."

"I agree with you there," Barnabas said. They were abreast of the great mansion now and he nodded towards the lawn and added, "It would appear that the good lawyer has arrived. I see his carriage."

She also saw the carriage and she noticed that the knot of people which had been surrounding the unfortunate gardener's body had also dispersed. She decided the corpse must have been removed.

"They are probably inside talking to your father," Barnabas said as they walked towards the front entrance of Collinwood.

"I'm almost afraid to hear what they may have to say," she confided.

He smiled at her and closed his hand reassuringly on her arm. "Didn't you make up your mind to face this bravely?"

"I know," she sighed.

Still her nervousness and misgivings continued as they entered the mansion. No sooner had they stepped into the shadowed entrance hall than she heard the high-pitched voice of the lawyer droning along from the direction of the living room. She gave Barnabas a glance of despair and he returned a look of amused resignation.

They went on into the living room. Her father was standing near the wide doorway facing a semicircle which included Lawyer Saul Hampstead, a rather stupid-looking man in a policeman's uniform, and the ancient Captain Westhaven. Everyone turned to stare at them as they entered and conversation ceased for a moment.

Hampstead finally came to sourly greet them. He scrutinized Barnabas with annoyance. "No one told me you had returned."

Barnabas smiled. "I had no idea you wished to be kept informed of my movements or I'd have let you know."

The lawyer frowned. "You need not be so saucy in your tone, Barnabas Collins. There is some question whether you're wanted back here."

"I don't anticipate any complaints," Barnabas said. "Unless you have one."

Hampstead turned crimson. "I'm surprised to find you out during the daylight hours. I have always known you to favor the darkness."

Barnabas had a certain cool arrogance as he replied, "You'll not be able to use that against me on this visit. I'm in excellent health and able to come and go when and where I please."

Lawyer Hampstead took a deep breath. "I'll have something more to say to you later," he told Barnabas. "For the moment we are occupied with the question as to how that gardener met his death."

Captain Westhaven, who'd been leaning on his cane in silence, now spoke up, "There's no mystery about it any more than there is a mystery as to what tore the throat of my sheep open!"

"I can't agree that there is any relation between the two happenings," Gerald Collins protested.

Lawyer Hampstead gave him a stony look. "I feel there is. Your lands are adjoining. The thing that did one killing very likely did the other."

"And I saw it!" Captain Westhaven said in a triumphant tone.

"I fear the evidence is strong against you, Mr. Collins. You have put us all in danger. Tell us what you saw the evening your sheep was killed, Captain Westhaven," Hampstead ordered.

Leaning heavily on his cane, the old man said with satisfaction, "I saw something flying away from where it happened. It looked like a thick snake about three or four feet long but it had a brilliant plumage and it soared up in the air like a bird!"

CHAPTER 8

Irma carefully watched Captain Westhaven as he told his story and she at once felt he was lying. He was much too glib in his recital of the description of the monster. It had to be a plot between him and the unscrupulous Hampstead, yet there was the shocking fact that the gardener had been found with his throat ripped open.

Hampstead cleared his throat. "Thank you, Captain," he said in his reedy voice. "I'd say that proves beyond any question what we're dealing with."

"It's fantastic!" Irma's father declared.

"It's natural for you to pretend innocence but under the circumstances we must assume you did bring some monstrous thing here and loosed it on our community. The constable will proceed on this belief and try and capture whatever it is," Hampstead told him.

Barnabas spoke up. "I don't think you can assume so much on what the captain has said. He's a very old man and liable to be confused under stress." Turning to an irate Captain Westhaven, he continued. "Isn't it possible that you exaggerated some ordinary bird into this weird flying monster? Your nerves were upset at finding your sheep killed and your eyesight is not what it was when you were younger."

The squat old man glared at him. "My eyesight is good

enough to spot someone tainted with the vampire curse!"

Barnabas didn't flinch. "That is not an answer to my question."

"He is not required to answer your questions," Hampstead said. "We will be on our way now. But when more is found out about this flying menace I will return." He nodded to the constable, and he, Captain Westhaven and the seemingly mute and confused village police officer made their way out.

When they had gone, Irma's father turned to her and Barnabas with a hopeless air.

"You can see what is going on," he said. "It's a plot to force me into selling Collinwood to them."

"Don't let them frighten you into any hasty action," Barnabas advised him. "They may create a lot of gossip and suspicion, but I doubt if they'll be able to come up with any concrete evidence you're to blame for the gardener's death."

Irma couldn't hide her fear. "But he was killed in such a hideous fashion!"

"I haven't any idea how it happened," her father said.

Barnabas gave him a very direct look. "It is your firm contention that no creature you brought here has escaped or bears any resemblance to this flying serpent?"

Her father nodded. "That is so."

"In which case you have nothing to hide or fear," Barnabas Collins said. "I have only just arrived but as soon as possible I'll do some investigating. I know many people in the area and it may be that I'll come up with something."

"Thank you," Professor Collins said sincerely. "All this has been so upsetting that I'm far behind in my cataloging."

Irma saw Barnabas out to the steps. She looked up at him and said, "You're very kind. Thank you for all you've tried to do."

"I want to help if I can," he told her. "I've had my own troubles with Lawyer Hampstead and I don't want to see Collinwood pass into his hands."

"I can appreciate your feelings," she agreed.

He frowned slightly. "It's difficult to say, but I hope your father is being completely honest with us."

"So do I."

"Only time will tell, of course," Barnabas said. "I'll see you again later after I've talked with a few people." Irma remained on the steps as he walked off in the direction of the old house. He was an impressive figure in his caped-coat and carrying his cane. He was also handsome in an odd fashion. It seemed to her he was one of the most interesting men she'd ever met. In comparison to him Stuart Jennings seemed no more than a callow youth.

Her mind was in a confused whirl when she went upstairs to her bedroom to have some time alone. She needed quiet to try to think things out. So much had taken place in no more than a few days. The murder of the gardener was the most shocking happening thus far and again she felt that her feelings of apprehension when she'd first entered Collinwood had been well-founded.

From the moment she stepped into the shadowed entrance hall she'd felt that danger lurked for her in the grim old mansion. As she'd moved from room to room in her inspection of it, the ominous forebodings had gained in strength. Too many members of the Collins family had known heartbreak and horror under this roof. There had been too many instances when a Collins had been placed under some dark shadow or had been cursed by a bitter enemy!

Their enemy at present was Lawyer Hampstead, but Irma felt it went far beyond that—that actual phantoms of the restless and unhappy dead must roam the dingy corridors in the midnight hours and somehow influenced those in the house in a devious fashion.

She hesitated at the top of the stairs and shuddered. It wasn't any good to speculate on how the gardener had come to his violent end. The very atmosphere of the place was charged with evil. She wished they could leave the house and the village at once. All her illusions of possible happiness in this setting had been shattered from the moment her father had dragged back all those repulsive live specimens with him.

But she hated to see the crafty lawyer win out over them. She had no special feeling for Collinwood such as Barnabas claimed, yet she did not want to see Hampstead get it for his own gain. She couldn't see how they could fight him with everything now going in his favor. Perhaps Barnabas might be able to help. He seemed a strong, assured person. But it could only be a hope, nothing more.

Irma noted that her bed had not been made or her room tidied up, but she put this down to the morning's upset. Crossing to the window, she gazed out at the grounds and the ocean beyond. Everything seemed quiet now on this dull, gray day. As she watched, Juan, in his white jacket, came from the direction of the stables and walked toward one of the side entrances of Collinwood that led directly to the cellar. She supposed he was kept busy supervising the specimens in both the stables and down there, not to mention the several crates on the rooftop, though it was all too likely one of them was empty now.

There was a knock on her door and she turned and said, "Come in."

It was Mrs. Branch who entered. The housekeeper seemed flustered. "What a disgrace that this room hasn't been done!" she sputtered. "I'm so ashamed!"

"It's all right," she said.

Mrs. Branch went directly to the bed and began making it. "I'll do it at once, Miss," she said. "Finding that poor man out on the lawn upset everything this morning."

Irma nodded. "I realize that."

"It's lost us one maid." Mrs. Branch said, sighing. "It may take a day or two to get another."

"One of the girls was frightened away?"

"Yes, miss. I tried to talk her out of it but I couldn't."

"Better to let her go."

"I told her it wasn't any of those creatures the professor brought back that killed the gardener but she wouldn't listen. She insisted some kind of awful feathered serpent was to blame." The housekeeper paused in her work. "Did you ever hear of such nonsense, miss?"

"The feathered serpent is an Aztec god," she said. "I suppose they've connected the legend with my father because we've just come back from the Mexican jungles."

"No doubt," Mrs. Branch agreed. "It doesn't take much to get them in a state. Silly girls!"

Feeling sick with despair, Irma turned to gaze out at the empty lawn once again and said, "The murder was a shocking thing."

"Yes, miss," the housekeeper agreed. "Do you suppose they have any idea who did it?"

"I don't think so."

Mrs. Branch came over to her and said, "I suppose I shouldn't be offering an opinion, but I wonder why they don't think of Louis when they're looking into the killing."

Irma stared at the woman. "Louis?"

"You wouldn't know him," Mrs. Branch explained. "He used to work here before the other owner died but he got sort of crazy. He had quarrels with most of the rest of the help, so they let him go. But he didn't travel far away from here. He has a shack down the beach a mile or so."

"And you think he's still around?"

"Yes. One of the stable boys saw him last week." She hesitated. "What I mean to say is that Louis always carried this nasty-looking knife on him. More than once he threatened to slash a throat or two around here."

"Why didn't somebody mention this when the authorities came?"

"I don't know," Mrs. Branch said. "They could have forgotten. It's been a long while since Louis worked here. But he wasn't right in the head and he did fight with the gardener just before the owner sent him away. I remember his language—it wasn't fit to repeat."

The woman's words had heartened her. "Do you think this Louis might have used his knife to slash the gardener's throat open?"

"Why not?"

"You think him that mad?"

"Yes, miss," the housekeeper said. "I wouldn't put anything past that Louis."

"Have any of the other servants discussed this?"

"No, miss," the housekeeper said. "I guess maybe nobody liked to think about it."

"I'll mention it to my father," she promised.

"I've only spoken of it because there has been so much other wild talk," the woman said in a worried tone. "Louis might have nothing to do with it. But at the same time you can't tell."

"I agree," Irma told her. "And I think you did right to mention it."

It brought her some relief. Shortly afterward she went downstairs in search of her father but was unable to locate him. Thinking he might have gone down to the cellar, she found the doorway leading to it and made her way down into its murky depths. Only a trickle of light filtered in through narrow windows which were scattered at long intervals and thick with the accumulated grime of years.

Irma felt uneasy down there but she was anxious to see her father. She went a long way in the near darkness before she saw the outline of a man ahead of her in the shadows.

"Is that you, Father?" she called out, halting at the same time.

"Miss Collins?" she recognized Jim Davis's voice.

"Yes," she said. "Is my father down here?"

The sailor limped over to her. His bearded face was grinning and his one eye fixed on her as he said, "He was but he left."

"Oh?" she said. "Have you any idea where he has gone?"

"No, miss. He didn't say."

"I see," she said. She continued to feel uneasy. There was something about the elderly sailor she didn't like. "Well, if he comes back tell him I'm looking for him."

Jim nodded. "I saw the captain here a while ago," he said with a harsh chuckle.

"Yes. He was here when Lawyer Hampstead came to

investigate the killing."

"Old villain! He hasn't aged a day since I sailed under him," the sailor said. "I kept out of sight while he was around."

"I'd say that was wise," she said.

"I figured that way, miss," he said. "Once he saw me he'd know I was able to tell a story or two about him. That would be a kind of warning for him."

"Yes," she said. "Father undoubtedly would prefer to have you appear as a surprise witness."

The single good eye of the sailor registered a wink. "Jim Davis can think as fast as the next one," he declared.

"Are you making out all right with your work?"

"First class," he rasped. "I've just been checking that big crate back there. It has as good a collection of reptiles as you'd want to look at, being locked in that box for weeks hasn't hurt them any if you can judge by the way they squirm and wriggle! I wouldn't want to stick a hand down in it and have one of them fork-tongues dip into me."

The picture of the writhing box of snakes which he'd conjured made her feel ill. She said, "Just be careful that none of them escapes."

"You can depend on that, miss," the sailor assured her.

"I'll go back upstairs," she said in a muffled voice. She was in a panic being down there in the darkness with those horrors so near her.

"Miss!" The sailor called to halt her flight.

She paused and turned. "Yes?"

"About the gardener? Do you think they know what happened to him?"

She sighed. "I'm afraid there's no definite answer as yet."

Jim Davis limped a few steps closer to her and stood there crouched against a backdrop of shadows. His single eye gleamed and it struck her the eyes of those serpents in the box might have a glitter much like it.

In a softer tone, he said, "There's one of them crates on the rooftop empty. Juan won't talk about it. But do you suppose something got out of it?"

She felt as if she might faint. "I can't say," she murmured.

"I've heard some of the help talking about a kind of flying monster," he went on. "Some of them think it killed the gardener."

"I know."

"You ever see anything like that?"

"No."

"Juan won't tell me anything," Jim Davis said in disgust. "He probably knows about it but he won't talk."

She felt she couldn't breathe if she remained down there. "I'd forget about it if I were you," she managed.

"Whatever you say, miss," the sailor said in his hoarse, odd voice. "You know best."

Irma hurried on to the stone steps and up to the ground floor. She stood for a moment leaning weakly against the wall. Going down to the fetid atmosphere of the cellar had been a mistake and that strange one-eyed sailor frightened her. It had been a dismal experience.

She had an urge to hurry to the old house and talk to Barnabas about what she'd heard. But then she remembered that he had spoken of visiting around in the area to try and get some information. The chances were all against his being there, so she settled for going up to her bedroom and trying to rest.

It wasn't until she went down to dinner that she saw her father. She thought that he was looking pale and ill, clearly showing the effects of the strain he was under. At once she told him of her conversation with the housekeeper, and he listened with what appeared to be relief. When she'd finished, he said, "It could be the answer."

"At last it gives us some logical basis for suspicion," she agreed.

"This Louis should be sought out and questioned," her father said.

"I think Barnabas would be the ideal person for that," she suggested.

He frowned. "Why Barnabas?"

"Because he knows the people here and the area generally. He'd have an idea exactly where to find him."

Her father looked more worried than before. "I hope you aren't allowing this Barnabas to charm you. He has the reputation for placing young women under his spell and using them."

"Nonsense!"

"You would be wise to be cautious," her father warned.

"Barnabas is probably the only true friend we have here."

Gerald raised his eyebrows. "What about Stuart Jennings? Are you forgetting him so easily?"

She looked down, a guilty flush mounting her cheeks. "Stuart is very nice but he's only a boy compared to Barnabas."

"He is not a hardened man of the world like Barnabas, you mean. Surely that is in his favor."

Her eyes met her father's. "Not in a case like this. We need the best brain and talent we can find to help us— which is what we can expect from Barnabas."

Professor Collins looked bitter. "I see that my judgment

doesn't impress you any longer."

She went up to her father with a wan smile. "It's you I'm thinking of mostly. That is why I feel you should allow Barnabas to join in helping us."

"If you insist," he said. "But there are some things in his own history that have never been sufficiently explained."

"You should be the last one to pay attention to rumors," she reproached him.

"He was in trouble here before," he said gravely. "There was his prowling around at night and then a couple of girls were attacked."

She closed her eyes and gave a small exasperated cry. "Father! I've heard all that story!"

"And you prefer not to believe it?"

"Just as I prefer not to believe the scandalous lies they are circulating about you!"

He looked shocked. "I don't see the comparison."

"Because you are too closely involved," she warned. "I say we should be thankful for Barnabas and accept any help he is willing to give us."

"As long as you don't become too personally interested in him," her father said.

She gave him a small smile and patted his hand. "Leave that to me to worry about."

It seemed to her that all during the dinner hour her father was not quite himself. She knew the shock of the gardener's murder had hit him hard, but he seemed even more upset than he had been in the morning. He ate very little, though he kept refilling his wine glass. Again she found a cold chill of fear surging back. Was this his way of confirming his guilt? Had he unleashed a monster to murder innocents?

She said, "You're hardly touching your food. What is wrong?"

He stared glumly at his plate. "My head aches."

"Perhaps the wine will help."

"I hope so," he said.

He was still withdrawn and strange when they left the dining room, and Irma was pleased when she saw a carriage coming up to halt before the front entrance of the mansion. In addition to a coachman, there were two other men alighting from the carriage. One of them was Stuart Jennings. The distinguished, white-haired man with him she took to be his father.

She was at the door to greet them. Stuart, hat in hand, smiled at her and introduced her to his father. The elder Jennings was more severe in looks than his son. His hair was silver rather than fair and he wore a well-tailored gray suit.

"Is your father at home, Miss Collins?" the elder Jennings asked her.

"Yes," she said with a smile. "Please come into the living room."

As they walked along, Stuart said, "I was away for a day. I just heard about your gardener. A distressing business."

"It's been a dreadful day," she admitted.

The elder Jennings frowned. "Bad luck seems to have dogged Collinwood in recent years."

When they joined her father in the living room Irma saw that the two elder men were stiffly formal in their greetings. She guessed that Stuart's father had come to discuss the disputed lumber land boundary, a fact which was borne out after a few minutes.

Her father turned to her, "If you and young Mr. Jennings will excuse us, his father and I would like to discuss some business in my study."

"It shouldn't take too long," the eider Jennings said. "There are some maps in there we wish to consult."

"Please go ahead with it," she told them, and with a smile for Stuart, she added, "I'm sure we'll have no problem filling in the time."

"Certainly not," Stuart agreed, looking pleased that they were going to have some privacy.

The older men left the room, their voices trailing behind them as they went down the hallway to the study. In the soft candlelight of the living room Stuart smilingly studied her, then came forward and took her in his arms for a kiss.

"You're lovelier than I remembered," he said, his arms still around her.

"Please," she said, pushing him away. "It's not the right moment."

Mild surprise showed on his boyish face as he released her. "Why do you say that?"

She shook her head. "So much has happened today. You have no idea."

"I'm sorry," he apologized. "I forgot about that for a moment. It was so good to be with you again."

She smiled at him faintly. "It's all right. Let's sit down somewhere. I feel exhausted and it's not because I'm physically weary."

"You've been under a great strain," he said solicitously. They sat on a divan near the fireplace. Irma told him about the discovery of the gardener's body and what had followed.

"Lawyer Hampstead is going to make it as bad for us as possible," she worried.

"I don't question that," Stuart said, "but there may be some solution to the murder besides the one he's trying to force on everyone."

"I hope so."

Stuart frowned. "By the way, when we were driving in just now I saw a weird figure limping along the roadway, a stranger I've never seen in Collinsport before. Rather formidable looking with gray hair and a whisker and a black patch over one eye."

"That's Jim Davis," she said.

"Jim Davis?"

She nodded. "Father hired him yesterday."

"Do you know anything about him?"

"Not too much."

Stuart sounded concerned. "He looks like a ruffian to me. I'm not sure your father used good judgment in employing him."

"I was there when it happened," she told him. "I think it is all right. The man is not as frightening as he looks, though I admit I'm not fond of him. Father hired him for a special reason."

"What reason?"

"At one time this man was a sailor who sailed under Captain Westhaven. According to him, he has some documentary evidence that Westhaven was in the slave trade."

Stuart's eyes widened. "That is interesting!"

"Have you heard this before?"

"Everyone has guessed that Westhaven was mixed up in some dirty business," Stuart said. "But no one knew for sure. He has put on a pious front since he retired and came back here to live. I can agree he's the right type to have owned a slaver."

"Jim Davis hates him and he offered to testify against him for father at any time," she said.

"Do you think it's just a bluff on the part of this Davis to get himself an easy job?"

"I certainly hope not."

"Your father didn't ask to see this proof?"

"No. Davis told him he'd had a lot of experience in handling animals and that settled it. Father felt that Juan needed a helper."

"Well, I hope it's as good as it sounds," Stuart said reluctantly, but Irma could tell he was far from convinced about the wisdom of hiring the sailor.

"We've also had someone else here," she went on. "Barnabas Collins is back."

This seemed to really surprise the young man. "Barnabas is back?"

"Yes. He came and introduced himself this morning."

"You have had an eventful day!"

"I told you."

He eyed her with some skepticism. "Are you certain it was the Barnabas Collins? He never appears in the village in the daytime."

"He explained that," she said. "It was because of an illness but now he is better."

"You have nothing but surprises for me!"

"He stayed a while and met Father. I think he is very nice."

"You'll get some arguments about that too," the young man warned her.

"I've heard those stories and I don't believe them," she said.

His eyes searched her face. "I'm sure you found Barnabas charming."

She blushed. "Of course. He's very nice."

"I've yet to hear any girl speak differently of him," he said wryly. "Yet there is much more about him than you can expect to know in a single meeting."

"I'm sure of that."

"So later you could change your mind," Stuart said, then added with a bitter smile, "Of course, I'm jealous."

"Nonsense!"

"Seriously, I am," he insisted. "If Barnabas decided to steal you from me I wouldn't have a chance."

"I hardly know him—we only met this morning!" she protested.

Stuart sighed. "I can tell you're not likely to forget him soon," he said.

Their conversation was interrupted by the return of their parents. Irma at once had the impression that the discussion between the two older men had not gone too well. They both seemed somewhat perturbed and the elder Jennings was eager to leave, so she had only a brief moment more with Stuart before the two men left in the carriage.

Standing with her in the darkness by the carriage, Stuart spoke low in her ear. "Be careful of Barnabas," he warned. "Don't let him steal your heart."

"You needn't worry," she protested, but she was thankful for the dark that hid her flaming cheeks.

Her father stood by her side as the carriage rolled away. He said, "I like young Jennings, but his father is very overbearing. He insists that Collinwood lumber cutters have been taking timber from his property, yet according to the map we consulted, they remained within our boundaries. He has promised to show me another map, which he claims is the correct one."

She said, "He may be difficult but I think he'll be fair."

"I hope so," her father said, as they stood there side by side a short distance from the house.

"Hadn't we better go in?" he asked.

"In a moment," she said. "You needn't wait for me. I just want to enjoy the air for a little longer."

"Is it safe for you?" her father asked in a worried voice.

"Of course," she said. "I'm not more than a dozen steps from the front door."

He sighed. "Very well. I want to go in and have another look at that map while the conversation is fresh in my mind," he said as he left her.

She remained there in the cool night thinking of her talk with young Jennings. It was ridiculous of him to have said she was becoming romantically interested in Barnabas. She hardly knew the charming Britisher, and yet he had made a definite impression on her.

Light from the downstairs windows of Collinwood sent a faint yellow beam to highlight the shrubbery a few feet away from her. Her eyes idly wandered to the neat hedge and then a stab of fear shot through her. She was seeing something which she could not accept!

CHAPTER 9

Gradually revealed on the top of the hedge was a thing so monstrous that Irma could not conceive of anything to equal it. The body was perhaps three feet long and at least seven or eight inches thick, becoming slimmer at the head and tail. Along this serpentine body were gaudily colored feathers extending out at least a foot, and the head had the glittering eyes and forked tongue of a snake!

Irma was too frozen with terror to move or even scream out. The eyes of the feathered serpent caught hers and she felt a kind of weird hypnosis taking hold of her. She knew that if she allowed herself to succumb to it she would be the next victim of the horrible creature. With a final frenzied effort she broke the spell with a sharp cry of fear. As she did so the feathered serpent raised from the hedge as if to come swooping after her.

Screaming and sobbing, she turned and ran the few steps back into the house to be met in the entrance hall by her startled father. He took her in his arms in an effort to comfort her. "I knew I shouldn't have left you out there," he scolded. "What is it? What happened?"

Between sobs, she managed to say, "The feathered serpent! I saw it!"

"You're hysterical!" her father told her.

"No! I saw it just now. It was on the hedge!"

"Let me see," Professor Collins said and, letting her go, crossed to the door and opened it. He stepped out into the darkness.

"Father! Be careful!" she cried and followed him.

He was standing just about where she had been and as she came to join him, he gave her a worried glance. "There's nothing on the hedge," he said. "Not a sign of anything."

She forced her eyes to concentrate on that spot again. Her father was right. There was nothing there. "I did see it! Right there!" Irma protested.

"This has been too strenuous a day for you," her father said, "and it was stupid of me to allow you to remain out here alone."

She gave him a distressed look. "You think I imagined it!"

"We won't argue about that now," he said wearily as he escorted her back into the house.

Inside, she persisted. "There was something on the hedge. It came after me as I started to run. It must have flown away."

Her father nodded. "There could have been some kind of night bird out there. Suppose we wait until the morning to discuss it."

She suddenly felt that exhaustion again. "Very well," she said quietly, much too weary to offer any further argument.

Her father went all the way to the door of her room with her and even waited to be sure that a candle had been lit and set out in her room. His mild face wore an expression of concern.

"You're sure you'll be all right now?"

"Yes."

"I don't know what you saw," he said worriedly. "But it was no feathered serpent."

Irma gave him a reproachful look. "Weren't we going to postpone any discussion until the morning?"

"I'm sorry," he apologized, then kissed her on the cheek. "Goodnight, my dear. Try to get a good rest."

She closed the door after him and bolted it. Then she crossed the room to the window and stared down at the lawn. She couldn't make out any sign of a moving thing in the darkness. All seemed quiet, and yet she knew that moment of terror had been real. That monstrous creature on the hedge was something she would never be able to forget. She comforted herself with the thought she would soon be seeing Barnabas and get his opinion and help.

Her sleep was troubled and not even a sunny morning did much to make her feel better. When she went down to breakfast her father greeted her more warmly than usual but she noticed that he made no reference to her scare of the previous night. Thinking this was the way he wanted it, she let it go at that.

After breakfast she was restless and went for a walk along the cliff path. The solitude and the pounding of the ocean on the shore below gave her a feeling of isolation. She attempted to go over the events of the previous day in her mind. She reached Widows' Hill and stood staring down at the rocks on the beach a dizzying distance below. This was where the lovely Josette had taken her life. Collinwood had always been a place of tragedy!

Turning away from the cliff's edge, she glanced back towards Collinwood and her heart gave a great leap as she saw a familiar figure striding across the lawns in her direction. Of course it was Barnabas! And he was a very welcome sight indeed! With a smile on her oval face and her hair streaming behind her in the slight breeze she hurried forward to greet him.

"I was going to the house when I saw you standing out here," he greeted her.

Irma gave him a plaintive look. "Oh, Barnabas, if you only knew how badly I've been wanting to talk to you. I was hoping you'd come."

He smiled, obviously pleased by her words. "Well, here I am. Now tell me all the secrets that have been bothering you." He took her hand in his as they began strolling back to Widows' Hill.

"I don't know where to begin!" she said.

"Start anywhere," he told her.

She began with her eerie experience on the lawn—of her certainty that she had seen the feathered serpent— and ended by saying, "Of course, Father said nothing about it this morning, so I feel sure he's guilty, that he did have that thing in a crate upstairs and it got away as Jim Davis claimed."

Barnabas seemed thoughtful. "It's easy to jump to that conclusion."

She was startled by his manner. "What do you mean?"

His glance was kindly. "Just what I said. You saw what you feel sure was some monstrous feathered serpent and your father avoids any discussion of it. This along with the other facts indicates that the monster exists and is free. It all adds up, but I'm afraid it's almost too simple an explanation."

"How can it be?"

"Let's allow just a small margin for error," he suggested. "You were nervous. It was late and the light wasn't good. There could have been some large bird out there which your imagination transformed into a monster."

"No!"

"I don't say that is how it was," Barnabas reasoned quietly. "I'm just using this as a possibility. Then we're still left in doubt about the monster and the murder of the gardener."

She was let down by his attitude but was sure he was sincere enough to be eager to do his best for her. So she asked, "What are you trying to make me believe?"

His handsome face showed a sad smile. "I'm not trying to make you believe anything. I'm attempting to discover the truth about all this."

She remembered what Mrs. Branch had said to her and told him, "There is something else which may appeal to you more." With that she went on to explain about the discharged employee, Louis, whom Mrs. Branch considered to be mentally unstable and capable of murder, and who had a grudge against the gardener.

Barnabas showed great interest in the account. "I remember Louis."

"Was he mentally upset?"

"A strange fellow," Barnabas said. "I didn't realize he was no longer working for the estate."

"Mrs. Branch says he has a shack about a mile along the shore from here."

Barnabas nodded. "I have an idea where it is."

"Do you think it would be any use to try to talk to him?"

"It might."

Irma looked forlorn. "I'd hardly expect him to make a confession or anything like that if he were guilty, but we might be able to tell from the way he answers our questions."

Barnabas said, "I'll go visit him."

"Take me with you," she pleaded.

He frowned. "Suppose he gives his answers with that knife Mrs. Branch is so sure he always carries?"

"I don't mind the risk."

"I mind it for you."

"Please," she said. "This is very important to me. I'd like to see and hear this Louis so I can judge for myself about him."

Barnabas smiled at her indulgently. "I began to sympathize with your father," he said. "You can be difficult to handle at times."

"I don't give up easily when I'm very concerned," she admitted.

"Very well," Barnabas said. "Shall we walk? It's quite a way but we can get there more directly than by carriage."

"I don't mind walking."

His handsome face showed ironic amusement. "The beach

will be hard on your shoes and if the tide comes in before we make our return you may find those fine flowing skirts of yours dragging in the water."

She gave him a pert look. "In that case I shall lift them up."

"Some would consider that daring," he reproved her.

She answered him with impatience. "I'm sure you're laughing at me and teasing me. And at a time like this! How can you be so cruel?"

"Sorry," he said. "We'll have to walk back a distance to find a path down the face of the cliff to the shore." They finally came to the steep path descending the rocky cliff face and he assisted her down. She always felt secure when she was in his company. Though she had reprimanded him for teasing her, she had not been really angry with him. He was much too nice and considerate otherwise. They reached the beach and began the long walk to the spot where Louis's shack was supposed to be located.

Barnabas gazed out at the ocean as they walked. "The tide is just going out so we shouldn't have any problems on our return trip."

"You were trying to scare me so I wouldn't come," she accused him.

"I'd be happier if you hadn't," he told her.

"Don't you like my company?"

"Very much."

"Then, why?"

"You know why. You could be placing yourself in danger."

She sighed. "I don't really think Louis has any part in what has been happening at Collinwood. He's probably not nearly so dangerous as Mrs. Branch thinks."

"She should know him well."

"Everything seems to get exaggerated," Irma complained.

He smiled faintly. "Keep that in mind when you tell your own stories."

"You don't believe anything I tell you!"

"I believed in this story about Louis enough to be making this long walk," he pointed out. "By the way, you mentioned that young Jennings and his father were over to visit you last night, but you didn't tell me what was said."

"Mr. Jennings and my father had some argument about woodland boundaries."

"What about you and Stuart?"

She shrugged. "We just talked."

"You don't want to tell me."

Irma was embarrassed. "It wasn't of any importance."

"I see," Barnabas said quietly. "I'm sorry. I didn't mean to intrude on your privacy. Stuart is a fine young man."

She looked at him reproachfully. "Don't make so much of it, Barnabas. We're really only casual friends."

"Your reticence about him suggests more than that," he warned her.

"You're wrong," she said. "Let us talk about something else. About you!"

Barnabas smiled in his melancholy way. "I may not want to go far with that subject."

"You will to please me," Irma insisted as he gave her his hand to help her over some rocks that blocked their way along the beach. When they had passed this hurdle she continued, "How does it feel to have your health again? After not being able to go about freely in the daylight for years, you're now walking in the sunshine with me. What is it like for you?"

"Like stepping out of my grave," he said.

"It was really that bad?"

"People of the night lead a very limited existence," he said.

"I'm sure that's true," she agreed. "It must make it much easier for you to travel."

"The arrangements are not anywhere near as complicated as before," Barnabas said.

"Do you plan to remain at Collinwood long this time?"

"That depends."

"I hope you stay until all this is settled," she worried. "I don't dare to think what it would be like here without you."

He gave her a pleased glance. "Have I come to hold that much importance for you?"

"Yes."

He smiled. "Then I mustn't desert you."

They walked on and for a time said nothing, being merely content with each other's company. An occasional gull would come wheeling above them with its hoarse cries. The ocean was far out, revealing a wide expanse of gleaming sand. They rounded a bend and ahead she saw a series of shacks built up on a sloping hill from the beach.

"Does one of them belong to Louis?" she asked.

Barnabas nodded. "Yes. We'll have to find out which one."

"There's a man sitting in the sun in front of one of the shacks," Irma said. "You can ask him."

"That would be the simplest solution," Barnabas agreed. They changed direction and headed for the first shack.

An enormous fat man sat nodding in the sun on a large rock in front of the ramshackle building. As they came up to him he suddenly opened his eyes and stared at them in surprise. It was hard to tell his age, and his clothes looked as if they'd been rescued from a rag bag.

Barnabas spoke to him. "We don't mean to disturb you but we're looking for someone."

The fat man stared at him through slits of eyes. "Who?" he wheezed.

"Louis. The one who used to work at Collinwood."

"The third place down." The man sounded relieved.

"Is he home?" Barnabas asked.

"He's always home," the fat man said with disgust. "He's bedridden."

This came as a surprise. Irma and Barnabas exchanged glances. Barnabas thanked the man and they moved on to the third shack, which was about twenty yards away. Irma was beginning to think they had come on a fool's errand.

In a low voice, she asked, "What do you think?"

"Hard to say," Barnabas replied.

They reached the door of the shack and Barnabas knocked. After a long moment a weak voice invited them to come in. A heavy fit of coughing followed the invitation. Barnabas opened the door and hesitantly entered. Irma followed close behind. The stench of the place almost sent her reeling back.

"What do you want?" Irma peered into the shadows and barely made out a man stretched out on the floor in a far corner of the shack. A foul, dark blanket had been thrown over his swarthy, emaciated form. His eyes had the hollow feverish look of one very ill or a madman.

Barnabas said, "You don't remember me, Louis?"

"Why should I?" Louis demanded sullenly.

"I'm Barnabas Collins."

"Collins!" The sick man spat disgustedly to show his hatred of the name.

"We heard you were sick and came to see if there was anything we could do," Barnabas said tactfully.

"No Collins cares about me!" He indicated Irma with a scrawny hand. "Who is she?"

"The daughter of the new owner."

Louis laughed nastily and then was seized by a fit of coughing. As he gained his breath again, he said, "The new owner will have the same luck as the last one. There's a curse on every Collins!"

"You shouldn't carry your hard feelings on to include this girl," Barnabas reasoned. "She had nothing to do with your discharge from Collinwood."

The sick man's eyes gleamed with malice. "I know why you're here! It's not about my health! It's because that gardener was murdered! You think because I'm trapped here too weak to move I don't know what is happening! I know!"

"There was a murder at Collinwood," Barnabas admitted.

"You'd like to have me blamed for it, wouldn't you? But it won't work this time. You see how I am. You had your trip here for nothing! Both of you!" Louis jeered at them.

"We're sorry we bothered you," she said quickly.

"Sure you are!" Louis said with scathing sarcasm. "You're disappointed! I can see it in your faces!"

"We wish you no harm, Louis," Barnabas said quietly, and taking some bills from his pocket, put them on the table near him. "Perhaps that will be of some help to you."

"Collins blood money!" Louis shouted at them maniacally. "Get out of here! Both of you!"

Barnabas hastily escorted her out of the shadowed, dirty place. Outside they paused to take a deep breath and look around. The fat man had suddenly vanished.

There was no one in sight. They walked back down to the beach and began the long journey to Collinwood.

Not until they were some distance away did Irma ask Barnabas, "What did you make of that?"

"Either he's dying or he's one of the best actors I've ever seen," he replied.

"I know," she worried. "He was very realistic. That cough of his certainly was frightening."

"I'd say he's very ill."

"I don't see how he could pretend to be that sick," she said, "but he seemed to be strong enough when he told us to get out."

Barnabas raised his eyebrows. "You're right. It could have been the result of his anger or he might have betrayed himself. He could be shamming just to throw us off the track."

"And he did know about the gardener."

"That kind of news travels quickly."

She sighed. "We're not any ahead, are we?"

"I'm afraid not," Barnabas admitted. "Though we have seen Louis. I'd put him far down on any list of suspects. I doubt if he could get up on his feet."

"Which makes my theory that there really is a feathered serpent at large all the more likely," she said bitterly.

"I'm afraid so," Barnabas was much subdued.

"What other explanation can there be?"

"I'll have to think about that," he said.

Irma halted and looked up at him with fear shining in her

eyes. "I don't know what to do, Barnabas! I don't know how to face this!"

He took her trembling body in his arms and drew her close to him. His lips caressed hers ever so lightly, then he held her tight and spoke in her ear in a low voice, "It will be all right."

"How do I know that?" she said, her voice breaking.

"Believe what I tell you," he said. "Fight this weakness. There is no way to go but ahead. You have to see this thing through."

She listened as he repeated these assurances and held her until her fit of trembling passed. Then hand in hand they continued on along the beach. No more was said between them. No more was needed, and Irma realized now that Stuart Jennings had been much wiser about her feelings towards Barnabas than she had realized. She was in love with this charming cousin from England.

They reached the path which led up the cliffs to Collinwood, and there seated on a rock was Jim Davis. A knowing smile was on his bearded, dark-skinned face and his one eye mocked them.

"Nice day for a walk," the sailor said.

"Yes, it is," Irma ventured nervously, thinking that he must have seen the embrace between them. She wondered what he would make of it as she introduced the two men. "This is my cousin, Barnabas Collins."

Jim slid down off the rock and touched a forefinger to his temple as a greeting to Barnabas. "Glad to meet any member of the Collins family."

Barnabas was staring at him. "Haven't we met before?"

"No, sir. Not that I recall," the sailor said.

"There's something about you seems familiar," Barnabas said.

The sailor gave a rasping chuckle. "More than likely it's the eye patch, sir. Put a black eye patch on any two men and no matter how different their faces are they begin to look alike."

Barnabas nodded. "That's probably it. I hear you sailed under Captain Westhaven."

"I spent more time than I wanted under command of the old rogue!"

"We must have a chat about it one day," Barnabas said.

"Any time you like, sir," Jim said. "I can tell you more than one tale about him."

"Miss Collins says you have had experience with animals," Barnabas said. "How did you acquire it since you have apparently spent your life at sea?"

He chuckled again. "Now, that is a good question, sir. A good question. I'll tell you. For three years I worked on a ship that was in the trade of bringing wild animals back from Africa to the circuses in Europe, and we had long weeks when those creatures had to be taken care of. The skipper didn't want no harm to come to that valuable cargo, so we had to learn how to look after them."

"I hadn't thought of that," Barnabas said, smiling faintly. "It would seem that Professor Collins was lucky to find you."

"And I'm happy with my job, sir," Jim said. "And it won't make me mad at all if I get a chance to even a score or two with that old rogue Westhaven!"

They left Davis on the beach and made their way up the path. On the way up, Irma whispered, "I'm sure he saw me in your arms."

Barnabas smiled at her. "Seafaring men are broadminded about such things."

She blushed. "It still is embarrassing."

"He's a strange type," Barnabas observed as they reached the top of the cliff.

"I agree that he is weird," Irma said, "but I think he is dependable."

"He is a ready talker, that's certain," Barnabas said. "Later on I will question him about Westhaven. I know something about the old rogue's history. I'll be able to tell whether Davis really knew him or not."

"That's a good idea," she said. "Will you come in and have lunch with us?"

Barnabas halted on the lawn. "Not today. I still have a few things to do."

She gave him a wistful look. "We don't seem to have much time together."

"We had a long walk."

"With no results."

"Don't be too certain of that," Barnabas said. "If all goes well I'll come over this evening."

She smiled. "That sounds better. What time?"

"After dinner. It is only lately that I have partaken of a full evening meal and my servant, Hare, enjoys preparing it for me. The poor fellow gets in a pique if I don't eat at home."

"Then we'll expect you later in the evening," she said. They parted and Irma went on to Collinwood. The day passed without event and she found herself anxiously waiting the return of Barnabas. She had told her father he would be coming and he'd seemed pleased. In fact he was in a much better mood than he had been earlier in the day.

After dinner they went to the living room and he insisted she join him in a glass of port wine.

"These tensions are making us forget the pleasant things of life," he complained. "We mustn't allow that. Before we are finished Collinwood shall become the home you dreamed about."

She smiled sadly over her glass of tawny port. "I'm afraid it's too late for that. I've taken a dislike to this house."

"Nonsense!" he said grandly. "I have been thinking about young Jennings' suggestion. It would be an excellent idea to hold a ball here and invite everyone for miles around. It might break the spell!"

She was stunned by his changed mood and couldn't help reproaching him by reminding him, "Father, how can you talk of having a party here when so short a time ago a man was murdered on our lawn. And his murder has not been explained."

Gerald Collins swallowed hard. "I haven't forgotten," he said soberly, "but I do not believe that murder had any connection with this household. I think the gardener must have had some enemy who attacked him out there. We cannot be blamed for that."

"And Captain Westhaven's sheep which was killed in the same way?"

Her father frowned. "I know that is a trumped-up lie conceived by that scoundrel Hampstead to make it seem I have released a monster to prey on the village."

"I wonder," she said.

At that moment Mrs. Branch entered. "One of the stable men is at the back door, sir," she told the professor in a troubled voice. "He wants to know where Juan is. He was supposed to be at the stables to look after the animals long ago and he hasn't shown up yet."

Her father looked surprised. "I can't imagine where he is. Juan is always reliable."

"I know, sir," Mrs. Branch said. "What will I tell the stable man?"

"Tell him I'll locate Juan and see that he gets right over there." As the woman left to deliver his message he turned to Irma. "I'd better go down to the cellar and see if he's down there."

Her eyes were filled with fear. "He may have been hurt. One of the snakes may have bitten him!"

Her father shook his head. "Jim Davis has been in charge of the reptiles since I hired him. He must be around somewhere."

"Be careful!" she pleaded.

Professor Collins sounded annoyed. "There's nothing

seriously wrong—just some delay or other."

He started to leave for the cellar but Irma called after him. "Take a candle with you."

"All right. Don't worry! Nothing is wrong!" he said curtly and went on out.

Irma stood there and watched him walk away, sick with apprehension, certain they were about to experience some new horror.

CHAPTER 10

Irma was still standing in the softly lighted living room when the knock came on the front door. She was in such a tense state she gave a start at the unexpected sound. Then she quickly went to the door and opened it. To her great relief it was Barnabas.

"I was beginning to wonder if you'd come," she told him.

He came inside. "Something delayed me." Then he stared at her. "You're looking very pale."

"We appear to have another problem."

"What now?"

"Juan seems to have disappeared."

He frowned. "Juan?"

"Yes. You have seen him. The Mexican whom father brought back to take charge of the live specimens."

"I remember," Barnabas said. "He's a thin, small man with white hair."

"Yes. He was supposed to be at the stables to give the animals their evening care and he hasn't shown up."

"What about the other man? The sailor?"

"He's been in charge of the things in the cellar, mostly the reptiles. Father has gone down now to see if Juan is with him. There may have been some temporary crisis down there that has delayed him."

Barnabas said, "It doesn't sound like anything serious, but you seem to be taking it badly."

"I am worried," she said, "and I'm glad you're here."

His gaunt, handsome face showed sympathy. "You've been under too much strain for too long a time."

"I agree with you in that," she said, as they stood in the semi darkness of the entrance hall. "All the months we spent in Mexico I wanted to get away. I was frightened of the jungle and the strange creatures inhabiting it. When we left I looked forward to coming here—at least I did until I discovered that Father was bringing a menagerie along with him."

Barnabas sighed. "It shouldn't take him too long to finish cataloging them and then he can send them on to zoos."

"I'd hoped that would be the way it would turn out," she said, "but so many things have happened since we arrived here. He's been held up in his work, and if anything is wrong with Juan I don't dare think how we'll make out."

"It's probably nothing to worry about," Barnabas comforted her.

"I hope not," she said, but she had no conviction in her tone. From the moment she'd arrived at Collinwood she'd felt under a dark shadow.

There were footsteps in the corridor and they both turned to see her father coming towards them. He was almost running, and his expression was troubled.

"Juan isn't down there. Jim is there alone. He claims he hasn't seen Juan since early this afternoon," the professor told them.

"Then where can he be?" Irma asked in dismay.

Her father sighed. "I don't know. I can't understand it."

"Would he leave without notifying you?" Barnabas asked.

"Where could he go?" Gerald Collins said. "He has no friends here. No means of transportation other than to walk. And why should he leave?"

"Something is wrong," Irma said.

"There is just one other possibility," her father said tensely. "He may have gone up to check the crates on the rooftop and taken ill up there."

She'd forgotten that some of the specimens were still up in the Captain's Walk. She said, "You should visit the roof at once!"

"I'm going to," he said, moving towards the stairway.

"I'm coming along," Irma told him as she followed him.

Her father turned. "Perhaps you'd better wait."

"No," she said. "My nerves are too much on edge. I can't bear the suspense."

"I'll come along as well, if you don't mind," Barnabas said

quietly.

Gerald Collins looked uneasy. "Very well," he said. "But there's really no need to make all this fuss. I'm sure Juan will turn up safe and well."

"Then it won't do any harm for us to go up there with you," she said.

The three of them began mounting the stairs. As they approached the various levels it seemed to Irma that the tension grew. Her father carried a candlestick with a good-sized candle to light the way up the dark stairways.

At last they reached the attic level and the last short flight to the Captain's Walk. Her father hesitated and asked them, "Do you want to wait here?"

Barnabas shook his head. "No. We may as well go all the way."

They started up that last narrow, steep flight of stairs with her father leading the way, Barnabas following directly after him and Irma in the rear. She felt sick with fear as they reached the door leading out to the roof. She knew that within a few minutes the search would be settled one way or another.

It was dark as they stepped out into the cool night. The flame of her father's candle flickered ominously and he cupped a hand around it to keep it from being extinguished. Making his way over to the crates, he peered into the darkness for some sign of the missing Juan.

Then he suddenly froze where he stood, and in a taut voice ordered Barnabas, "Don't let Irma come over here!"

Her fear became panic. "What is it?"

"It's Juan," her father said. "He's dead! Behind the crates. His throat has been torn open—the same as the gardener's."

Barnabas put an arm around her and she slumped against him and began to sob gently. In a way she had expected it but now that her fears had become reality she found it a shocking experience.

Her father came back to them, his face ashen. "I don't know where this leaves us," he said in a hushed voice.

"May I have the candle?" Barnabas asked. "I'd like to take a look over there for myself."

Professor Collins said nothing but held out the candle for him to take. Barnabas went across the Captain's Walk, leaving Irma with her father. She was trembling and couldn't seem to stop.

"Poor Juan!" her father murmured.

She gave him an accusing glance. "Now can you say you still feel no responsibility?"

"How could I predict this would happen?"

Irma said, "You knew you had brought that monstrous thing back here and it had gotten free!"

"No!" her father protested.

Barnabas looked solemn when he came back. "I took a close look at Juan's hands. I found these two or three torn feather ends clutched in one of them." He opened his hand to disclose the fragments of feathers in his palm.

"That proves there is a feathered serpent," Irma declared as she turned to her father. "Do you still deny it?"

"Yes."

"How can you?"

Her father's face had taken on an older, wearier look. "If there was such a creature included among the specimens it was without my knowledge."

Barnabas stared at him. "Would that be possible?"

"Yes," he said. "Juan could have found a specimen of this legendary creature and taken it on himself to crate it and include it with the other items. I wouldn't have noticed the extra crate."

This was a new light on a perplexing problem. The thought that Juan alone might be responsible for the feathered serpent had never occurred to her. Now she saw that it was possible. She also realized this could be a clever diversion on her father's part to escape blame and shift it to the dead Juan. Juan would not be able to dispute him.

"I hope you are being completely honest in this," she said.

"Why should you doubt me?" her father asked plaintively. "Have I ever engaged in criminal acts against society before? Why should I now?"

"It's just so convenient," she said. "I mean, to have you partially accept the idea there is a feathered serpent at large and place the blame on Juan."

"It is because Juan has died as he has that I'm forced to think about a monster looking for victims," her father said. "I'm still dubious such a thing as a feathered serpent exists."

"There's a lot to be explained," Barnabas told them. "It would seem you'll have to contact the authorities, and that means subjecting yourself to the not-so-tender mercies of Hampstead once again."

"Do we have to call him back here?" Irma asked dolefully.

"I'm afraid so," Barnabas said.

Professor Collins glanced back through the night shadows to where the torn body of Juan was. "This is just what he wants. Be prepared to have him make the most of it."

"That won't come as any surprise," Barnabas said.

"What about the specimens?" she worried. "Who will take care of them now?"

"Jim will have to take over the major responsibility," her father said.

"It will be too much for him. He has that limp which makes him slow getting around," she worried.

"I'll help," her father said. "I'll go to the stables now. Later I'll train an assistant for him."

"Where will it end?" Irma lamented.

"That's something we can discuss downstairs," Barnabas told her. "There is no point in us remaining here."

"Barnabas is right," her father agreed.

"What about the creatures in the crates?" she asked.

"Apparently Juan saw to them before he was attacked," her father replied. "Up here we have mostly birds. I'll have another look at them later. Now I must notify Jim of what has happened and hurry to the stables with him."

Barnabas asked her father, "What do you have mostly at the stables?"

"The larger creatures," he said. "Lizards and some carnivorous animals. They are the ones that must be attended to promptly before they start cannibalizing." Irma shuddered and pressed close to Barnabas.

"Take me back downstairs," she said in a faint voice.

When they reached the ground floor, her father left them at once. Barnabas went over to the sideboard in the living room and poured her out a drink of some amber liquid. Then he brought it back to her.

"Sip this," he said. "It's strong but it will help sedate you."

She took the glass. "My head is throbbing."

"I know," he said.

She took a sip of the straight liquor, which burned her mouth and throat. "What now?"

Barnabas escorted her over to a high-backed chair and seated her in it. Then he began to pace slowly up and down in front of her. He said, "I'm beginning to think you are right about the feathered serpent, and that it returned to the rooftop from where it escaped and attacked Juan."

Over her glass she asked, "What about Father?"

"I heard what he said up there," Barnabas spoke quietly.

"Do you think he is telling the truth?"

Barnabas halted and looked at her solemnly. "I would like to think that he is."

"But you're not sure," was her bitter reply.

"How can we be sure at this point?"

"It's strange," she said. "Why didn't Father accept the possibility of there being a feathered serpent before?"

"I'd say he explained that satisfactorily," Barnabas said. "Only with Juan's murder did it seem likely to him."

"You found those scraps of feathers in Juan's hand!"

"Yes," Barnabas nodded. "I suppose Hampstead will make the most of that."

Irma was filled with a chilling fear. "Once the word of how Juan died gets out, the whole village will be in a panic!"

"There is no way of hiding the news from them," Barnabas agreed unhappily.

"Father will have to sell the property!"

Barnabas indicated the many portraits that hung in the double parlors. "How can he? He'd be turning his back on all these ancestors who helped build the family name and estate."

She finished the last of the burning liquid and felt some more assurance. "He'll have no choice, Barnabas, unless you want to take over the property and remain on here. He can't do it after the news has spread that he is an irresponsible villain!"

Barnabas was grim. "I'm in no position to assume responsibility for the estate," he told her. "For one thing, my own reputation is not too high in the village. And for another, I'd not be content to remain here. I have always been a wanderer and I shall likely always continue to be one."

She eyed him bleakly. "This would be the ideal moment for Quentin to appear. I'm sure he'd have nerve enough to take over the estate. From my knowledge of him he was bold enough."

"Brazen is the proper word," Barnabas said. "But not even his nerve would see him through this. His repute in the area is the worst of any. He can never return to Collinwood."

"So there appears to be no one to stand in the way of Hampstead," she mourned.

"Not unless we can prove that your father is innocent of any responsibility in these deaths," Barnabas said.

"That won't be easy," she said.

"Still, we shouldn't give up," Barnabas warned her.

She was about to question him further when Mrs. Branch ushered Stuart Jennings into the room. The fair haired young man took on a strained look when he noticed Barnabas.

Going over to Stuart, Irma said, "I'm glad you're here. This is Barnabas Collins. I'm sure you've met before."

"Yes, we have," the young man said as he and Barnabas shook hands.

Barnabas was perfectly cool and collected. "I think it was two years ago in the Blue Whale Tavern," he said.

"Possibly," Stuart said. She could tell that something was bothering him, and wondered if he'd heard about Juan.

She said, "There's been another violent death here. Have you heard about it?"

He looked stunned. "No!"

"Juan," she said. "We found him on the roof with his throat in the same state as the gardener's."

"When?"

"Just a little while ago. We haven't even sent word to the village yet. Or at least as far as I know, Father hasn't."

Stuart looked shocked. "That is dreadful!"

"Even Father now admits there may be some monster loose and threatening us," she said.

The young man nodded. "That is one of the reasons I'm here. One of the village women claims she saw a feathered serpent outside her window this afternoon."

She gave a small gasp. "When?"

"In mid afternoon," Stuart said. "I didn't place too much stock in her story since she happens to be Hampstead's housekeeper, but with what you've just said to me, it begins to seem more likely."

Barnabas was frowning. "Hampstead's housekeeper claims she saw this monster?"

"Yes. Supposedly when she was in the kitchen working, it came in view of a window. She saw it and screamed. The thing tried to get inside and did break the window-pane. Meanwhile she became hysterical and locked herself in a closet. When Hampstead returned to the house he found her there, and sent word to the local constable."

"Did this woman describe the creature?" Barnabas wanted to know.

"She did in a sort of way," Stuart told him. "She said it was a flying snake, a thick one, covered with bright feathers."

Irma nodded. "That sounds like the description of what I saw on the hedge. And none of you would believe me!"

"None of us wanted to believe you," Barnabas pointed out.

Stuart Jennings' eyes were wide with the excitement of it. "I put it all down to a wily stunt on Hampstead's part to get the villagers frightened. Now it seems he may have been telling the truth."

"No one will doubt it when they hear what happened to Juan," Barnabas said dryly.

Stuart turned to her. "If this thing is at large your father must have some thoughts about how to trap it or destroy it!"

"Father is just getting around to admitting it exists," she said wearily.

"Where is your father now?" Stuart asked.

"At the stables, taking care of the specimens. Juan never did arrive to do the evening chores."

Barnabas said, "I'm going to leave. I'll stop by the stables and talk to him for a moment before I go."

Irma faced him. "Must you leave so soon?"

"Yes," he said. "I'm going to the village. You don't need me now since you'll have Stuart for company."

"I'd rather you also stayed," she said, her eyes meeting his.

"Let me decide this time," he said quietly.

He bade Stuart Jennings goodnight and Irma saw him to the door. He placed his arm around her for a moment and said, "Hold fast to your courage," but he left without kissing her. She watched him walk off into the shadows with the feeling that the arrival of Stuart Jennings had made him uncomfortable. She worried that he'd been hurt by the appearance of the young man.

When she returned to the living room, Stuart gave her a knowing glance and said, "Barnabas rushed off very suddenly."

"I know," she said. "Perhaps he thought of something."

"Or did he resent my showing up?"

"Why should he?"

"He's fond of you, and he sees a rival in me."

Irma frowned. "This is hardly the time for that sort of talk with a murdered man up on the rooftop and the house in a panic."

"I'm sorry," he said. "I had to mention it."

"And I've told you my feelings," she said.

Stuart looked hurt. "Do you want me to leave as well?"

Irma looked at him helplessly. "That is up to you."

"I'll stay if I can do any good."

She turned away from him. "You could wait until you see Father. He no doubt will be anxious to hear your story first-hand." She wanted him to remain during this frightening period but didn't intend to plead with him to do it.

He came over to her and gently turned her to face him. "I'm sorry. I was behaving in a petty fashion," he said. "I'm jealous of Barnabas, as you know."

"Please!" she begged.

"I'll say no more," he said. He bent close and touched his lips to hers.

She was still in his arms when she heard someone clearing his throat near them. Drawing back from Stuart quickly she was startled to see Jim Davis standing there.

She said, "What is it, Jim?"

"I've been waiting for the Mister," he said. "I've finished my tasks downstairs. Would he want me at the stables?"

"I imagine so," she said. "You'd better go and ask him."

"Yes, miss," the sailor said, a strange glitter in his single eye and a leer on his face. "This has been a bad night. Juan was a marvel with the animals. It won't be easy without him."

"It won't," she agreed.

"Well," he rasped, "I'd best be on my way." With a nod he limped out of the room and vanished.

"That's a strange character," Stuart Jennings said, watching after him.

"We're lucky to have him with Juan dead."

"I guess so," he said, "but I don't think much of the way he sneaks around the house."

Irma knew Stuart resented their being caught in each other's arms, but she felt that the sailor could hardly be blamed for their behavior. She said, "I don't think he came upon us deliberately."

"No, of course not," Stuart said unhappily.

Professor Collins returned from the stables a half-hour later looking tired and old. He seemed glad to see Stuart and listened to his story about Hampstead's housekeeper and the flying serpent. When the young man ended his account, the professor sank heavily in a nearby chair.

"I hate to stain the memory of a dead man," he said. "But I'm forced to think that Juan brought this creature back unbeknown to me. It is a grim irony that he met his death from it."

Stuart said, "Have you any way of proving that?"

Her father gave him a bitter glance. "My word against a dead man's."

The young man considered. "There is your daughter. Irma can testify that you weren't aware of the serpent being in the shipment."

Irma's father gave her a strange glance. "Would you be willing to do that?"

She hesitated a bare second. "Yes, I suppose so. If I have to."

Her father smiled bleakly. "I note you are not enthusiastic, so apparently you still are suspicious of my role in all this. If you doubt me what chance have I of convincing others of my innocence?"

"I didn't say I doubted you," she said.

"Your tone implied it," he told her sadly.

"I'm sure you needn't worry about Irma's support," Stuart said. "And Barnabas will back up your story. He was present when you found Juan's body."

"And he'd just arrived at Collinwood as the gardener was discovered with his throat torn open," she said.

Her father raised his eyebrows. "Perhaps we should be careful about dwelling on that. The townspeople still are suspicious of Barnabas and they might take it into their heads that he is the killer."

Stuart looked solemn. "I hadn't thought about that."

"We do have one card up our sleeve when Hampstead and Captain Westhaven begin spreading their vile stories about us. We have Jim Davis to tell his account of the kind of business Westhaven was engaged in."

Stuart nodded. "That will help discredit anything they may say and turn attention from the happenings at Collinwood to that old rogue of a captain."

Irma asked her father, "Did you send word to the village?"

"Yes," he sighed. "I suppose we can expect Hampstead and that constable, who is no more than his lackey, to appear at any time."

As it turned out they arrived sooner than anyone expected. Irma was still sitting talking with Stuart and her father when the lawyer and the constable came.

Hampstead looked smug as he told Gerald Collins, "It seems that this monster has struck again. I doubt if even you can argue as to its existence any longer."

Looking crestfallen, her father said, "I'll take you up to the Captain's Walk where the body is."

When the three had gone up the stairway Stuart turned to Irma with a resigned expression. "It's evident that Hampstead is going to make this as unpleasant as possible," he said.

"I don't think we ever doubted that," she pointed out.

He glanced around the room at the various Collins family portraits. "In some ways you are right. This has never been a happy place. Nearly everyone whose likeness hangs on these walls had some problem or other. Down through the years various members of the family have suffered from some curse."

"I know."

He studied her seriously. "Perhaps you wouldn't mind giving Hampstead his way. Moving out of here wouldn't be a tragedy to you."

"Not any more. But Father and Barnabas seem to feel it would be breaking faith with the family to do so." Her father came back down the stairway with Hampstead, but the constable was remaining up on the roof with Juan's body until a wagon came to take it to the village.

Saul Hampstead was in one of his overbearing moods. His sunken eyes showed a malicious glow as he informed her father, "Unless this monstrous thing is captured and destroyed I shall hold you personally responsible for whatever happens."

Mr. Collins looked shocked. "But that is most unfair! I'm not ready to admit there is such a creature."

"I do not expect you to admit it," the lawyer said, smiling mockingly. "You have brought our village under a threat so horrible it is beyond the mind to conceive!"

"Suppose these murders were perpetrated in some other way," the professor argued. "We may have a murderer to deal with here, not a monster."

"It was no human killer my housekeeper saw from the window of the kitchen today," the lawyer told him. "She saw the Aztec feathered serpent which you so recklessly brought back here."

"That will have to be proven," the professor said.

Hampstead sneered. "I doubt if that will be difficult. Captain Westhaven also saw the monster when it destroyed one of his sheep."

"I spent months in the Mexican jungles," Gerald Collins said, "and I did not set eyes on anything such as has been described."

"I'll also ask you to get rid of the remaining specimens you have here. I don't care what you do with them, but I insist you remove them from the area," the lawyer ordered.

Professor Collins reacted with shock. "But I can't do that until I have finished my work with them. If I do, a large portion of my findings on the expedition will be lost."

The tall, spare lawyer smiled coldly. "I'm afraid that does not interest me, Professor Collins."

"You can't force me to do it," the professor said angrily. "There can't be any law to make me!"

"We'll find one, Professor, never fear," Hampstead said in his smug way. "Already you've lost any hope of being able to remain at Collinwood. The villagers will never forgive you for what you've done!"

CHAPTER 11

The weather was pleasant again the following day, but for Irma it was merely another day of tension after a night in which she'd managed little sleep. When sleep had come to her she'd had terrible visions of the feathered serpent. The monster had haunted her dreams. She went down to breakfast pale and shaken to find that her father had breakfasted early and gone off somewhere.

She went outside for a stroll in the sun and sat on a bench in the garden when she became tired. She hoped that Barnabas would come and worried that he might have been offended by the arrival of Stuart Jennings the night before. She liked both men but it was almost inevitable that Barnabas would be her favorite of the two.

While she was sitting there, Mrs. Branch came out to her with an apologetic air. "I'm sorry to bother you, miss," she said, "but I can't find your father."

"He's either at the stables or has gone to the village," Irma said. "In either case he should be back soon."

The housekeeper smoothed her white apron with her hands and said, "I'm having more problems with the help. Two of the maids and a kitchen girl are leaving this afternoon."

"That's too bad."

"Yes, miss, but after what happened to Juan and the

gardener, and the stories that are being told there's just no way of keeping them here."

"I can understand how it is," Irma said. "I'm surprised that we haven't lost more help."

Mrs. Branch looked worried. "There's talk that some of the stable workers are leaving at the end of the week."

Irma nodded. "Well, I suppose we'll manage somehow." She gave the woman a rueful smile. "I hope you aren't getting any such ideas."

"No, miss. I'm not afraid, though they do say that flying monster is hiding in the woods waiting for a chance to come back and murder another of us."

"That's a pretty lurid account of the situation," Irma said. "My father isn't sure there is such a thing as a feathered serpent."

"But people have seen it!" Mrs. Branch protested.

"I know," she sighed. "I even believe I saw it. But I could have been mistaken."

"Yes, miss. It's the killings and the brutal way they were done that really have frightened the folk around here."

Irma stared at the older woman solemnly. "Is the story spreading in the village? Is it really bad?"

"I'm afraid so, miss," Mrs. Branch said with a sad look. "They are saying some cruel things about the professor."

"They're very quick to condemn," Irma said.

"Yes, miss."

"But that has always been the case, hasn't it?" she said. "A number of the Collins family have been accused of dark acts by the villagers."

"That's true, miss," Mrs. Branch said. "But it's been different lately since Mr. Quentin left and hasn't come back. He was the one most people here feared. Then for a little while they thought Mr. Barnabas might not be what he seemed, but he's back again and appears as normal as anyone."

"I'm sure he is."

Mrs. Branch sighed. "And not too many years ago they had gossip going the rounds that he bore the same vampire curse as his ancestor. I never did believe it, though a lot of people claimed it to be true."

Irma rose with a sad smile. "So my father is not the first Collins to be feared by the local people."

"No, miss, you can be sure of that. Shall I try to get replacements for the girls that are leaving?"

"Not yet," she said. "I think it's a poor time to try and get help. Let us wait and perhaps the scare will end."

"Yes, miss," the housekeeper said respectfully and went on

her way.

Irma was not surprised to learn that the household staff were panicking. She had fully expected something of the sort. She didn't know where her father had gone or what he was doing, but she felt it might be connected with the project of destroying the monster. Feeling somewhat uneasy, she decided to walk to the stables and see if he might be there.

The sun was beating down and it was warmer than any other day. She left the garden area for the dusty roadway that led to the stables. As she approached them she saw a group of the help gathered in the door of the largest stable while out in the sun Jim Davis was standing with what looked to be a couple of giant lizards.

She was puzzled at this and became more so as she drew near to hear the laughing and guffaws of the help as they shouted to the sailor. The one-eyed man was moving around among the giant lizards which were about six feet long and at least two feet high. Occasionally he poked them with a sharp-pointed stick and they reacted by sluggishly moving and extending their forked tongues. He seemed unaware of her approach, but the stable boys saw her and at once quieted down, some of them vanishing inside the dark building.

Irma went up to the sailor and demanded, "What does this mean?"

He swung around with surprise on his bearded face. "Miss Collins!"

"What are you doing with these creatures, putting on some kind of an entertainment?" she asked with annoyance.

"No, miss," he said at once. "I thought since the sun was natural to them that it might do them good to be in it for a while."

She glanced at the scaly monsters with their clouded eyes. "That may be true, but some of them also frequent the dark, moist areas of swamplands. Unless one is sure of the type it would be wise to keep them in their crates."

"I'm sorry," the sailor said.

She studied the stick in his hand. "I don't approve of all that prodding either."

Jim Davis looked uncomfortable. "I needed something to handle them with, miss."

"I was watching you as I came here," she said with a reproachful glance. "I saw you tormenting these creatures to amuse the stable hands. Don't do it again."

"No, miss," he said, his tone contrite.

"Have you seen my father?"

"Yes, miss," he said. "He drove in to the village. I believe he wanted to make arrangements to send some messages by wireless to see about placing the animals."

"Thank you," she said. "Did he mention when he would return?"

"No, miss," the sailor said.

She looked at the ugly monsters there in the sun and said, "I also think it's best to keep these things out of sight at present. Some of the help are badly upset and not used to seeing species of this sort. These creatures look more dangerous than they are. They can only have a bad effect on the morale of the servants we have left."

"I'll take them in directly, miss," he promised.

"You have full responsibility in these things now that Juan is gone," she reminded him.

The sailor nodded. "That's right enough, miss," he said in his raspy voice. "I'll do my best."

She left him, hoping that this would be true, but the incident bothered her. Just as soon as her father was out of the way Jim Davis had begun taking liberties that he shouldn't have. He would have to be watched carefully since his judgment appeared to be faulty.

Without realizing it, Irma found herself walking on towards the old house where Barnabas was living. As she saw the red brick building loom in the distance she decided she would try to contact Barnabas. She wanted to be sure he'd not taken offense at Stuart's arrival the previous night and ask him for advice. More and more she was coming to depend on the handsome Britisher's opinions.

Reaching the entrance to the brick house she went up the steps and used the door rapper. It seemed an endless time passed before she heard footsteps approach in the hallway. Then the door was hesitantly pulled open and a broad face with a stubble of beard appeared in the dark slit of the doorway.

She assumed this was the servant, Hare, and smiled. "I'm looking for Mr. Barnabas Collins," she said.

The squat man made a grunting noise and shook his head.

"He's not at home?" She found the appearance and behavior of the man somewhat alarming.

Again Hare made a noise in his throat and shook his head.

"Where can I find him?" she wanted to know.

There was a slight hesitation on Hare's part, then he opened the door a little further to point a stubby forefinger in the direction of the cemetery.

She glanced at him questioningly. "The cemetery? He's gone to visit the cemetery?"

The servant nodded vigorously this time and made other throat sounds.

"Thank you," she told him. "I'll go and see if I can find him."

Hare quickly went back inside and shut the door hard; it seemed he wasn't too fond of visitors. She descended the steps and headed for the field leading down to the cemetery. Her last visit to the grave yard had not been too pleasant, but the prospect of discovering Barnabas there was irresistible. She was very anxious to discuss some things with him.

The field was deserted and she could see no sign of anyone moving around in the distant cemetery. But it was hard to tell so far and she knew that Barnabas could easily be in the rear of the iron-fenced area, hidden by the large monuments and shade trees. As she drew nearer the burial ground she began to have certain qualms. She worried that she shouldn't have ventured so far from the main buildings of the estate alone. But surely there was no danger as long as Barnabas was there.

But suppose the servant had been wrong and Barnabas wasn't there? The thought was so alarming it caused her to halt briefly and consider whether she should go on. Then her fears suddenly seemed ridiculous to her. It was a lovely day with the sun at its midday strength. Surely she needn't fear this sanctuary of the dead at such a time and under such conditions, she told herself as she resumed her journey to the burial ground of the Collins family.

She was uncomfortably warm, and the straw bonnet she was wearing had too narrow a brim to give her proper protection from the sun. She decided it was more of a nuisance than a help and untied its strings under her chin and took it off. She walked the rest of the way to the cemetery gates with it in her hand.

Once she stepped in among the gravestones the atmosphere seemed to take on a different character. There was a hush in the air and this brooding silence had an effect on her nerves. She moved along the path between the various headstones searching for a glimpse of Barnabas but she didn't see him. Again she began to worry that the servant had misled her.

It was too late to think about that now; she was already in the cemetery. She could only make the complete rounds of it, hoping the handsome Britisher would turn up. Before she knew it she was far back among the graves and had reached the section where the large tombs had been constructed. According to Barnabas, these family burial places had been the scene of much confusion over the years, so that now no one was sure which coffins had been transferred to which tombs. To top it all, there was the continuing rumor that one coffin might contain a quantity of precious jewels.

Irma moved from the shade of a giant elm to stand before the tomb in which the ancient Captain Westhaven had been lurking that other day, and to her amazement the rusty iron door of the tomb was again ajar. Had he returned to the underground room to continue his search for that casket with its treasure?

It angered her that the old man should so brazenly trespass on their grounds and attempt to plunder the casket of one of her ancestors. There was no other motive she could give to his actions. In her annoyance she temporarily forgot her fear or that the purpose of her visit to the cemetery had been to locate Barnabas.

Advancing to the worn, moss-covered stone steps leading to the dark entrance of the tomb she leaned down and called out, "Are you in there, Captain Westhaven?"

Of course there was no reply. Even if he were again guilty of this audacious conduct he wasn't liable to admit it by answering her, but she had the feeling she had caught him red-handed. Who else would have opened that tomb door? Still impelled by anger, she advanced down the several steps and, crouching a little to clear her head, went into the shady darkness of the tomb.

It took her a moment to accustom her eyes to the dark. Then she saw that she was in a fairly big room, square in shape, and at the end of it there were shelves from floor to ceiling divided in perhaps a dozen sections. Each section contained a dust-ridden casket.

The strong aroma of dampness and decay was overpowering in the shadowed place, but there was no sign of the old man in there. She strained her eyes, staring into the darkest corners to make sure. Except for the dead in their coffins the place was empty. Having satisfied herself of this, she started toward the doorway through which a narrow path of sunlight beamed. She was barely a half-dozen feet from it when she heard an eerie sound.

It was the kind of sound she had always thought a rattlesnake must make, and it was coming not from under her feet where she might have expected it, but from the entrance way of the tomb. She halted, terror temporarily gripping her in a paralysis. The sound came ominously again from the steps leading into the tomb. Her horror was complete as she realized she had placed herself in a position where she could easily be trapped.

She waited. The sound wasn't repeated. What to do? She couldn't remain in that fetid underground place of the dead, so she forced herself to move on a few steps. And then she saw it and she cried out her fear!

Hovering in the entrance of the tomb was the brilliantly plumaged feathered serpent. It swayed from side to side as it made that weird sound again. Irma raised her hands over her face to shut off the horrifying spectacle and she screamed over and over!

From a distance, almost like a faint echo, she heard her name called, "Irma!"

At once she cried, "Here! Here in the tomb! Help me!"

"Irma!" Her name came again in the resonant tone of Barnabas.

She lowered her hands slowly from her face and made herself gaze at that doorway. The feathered serpent had vanished!

"Irma!" Barnabas shouted to her again, nearer this time, and a moment later he showed himself at the entrance of the tomb and came down to get her.

"The serpent!" she sobbed as he took her in his arms.

"What about it?"

"I came down here and it trapped me. It was in the doorway. Didn't you see it?"

"No," he said, "let me get you out of this place!"

He quickly escorted her out of the tomb and up the steps into the open. She leaned against him weakly. It seemed every ounce of strength had drained out of her. At last she said, "I saw that monster clearly. There's no doubt about its existence anymore. It must be hiding somewhere in the cemetery!"

Barnabas glanced around them. "I can't imagine why I didn't see it."

"My screams may have scared it off," she suggested.

"I doubt that," he said grimly.

She now was recovering. "It has to be somewhere close at hand."

He frowned at her. "Why did you come here?"

"I went to your place. Your servant indicated you were here."

"He was wrong," Barnabas said. "I walked in this direction but I took a stroll through the woods to the swamp first. Then I fortunately decided to stop by here on my way back."

"I couldn't move in there until I heard your voice," she said.

"Why did you go in there?" Barnabas asked.

"I found the iron door open again, and knowing that Captain Westhaven had been in there the other day, I suspected he was down there once more."

"And he wasn't."

"No."

Barnabas said, "Probably he was there and left. He seems to have a habit of not closing the door after him. I think he's mad."

"I'd only been in there a few minutes when I heard an odd sound, a kind of hissing-rattling sound. It was the feathered serpent!"

"So now we know," Barnabas said. "You saw it in daylight."

"Yes."

Barnabas looked concerned. "The first thing I'd better do is get you safely back to Collinwood. I'll speak to your father and then organize some kind of group to search this area and the woods to try and rout out that monstrous creature."

"Father was in the village when I left Collinwood but he'll probably have returned by the time we get back," she said.

"I hope so," Barnabas said. "I'd like his suggestions in organizing the hunt."

She said, "That thing must be destroyed. It will always haunt me!"

His arm was around her. "Try and blot what you saw out of your mind."

"I'll try," she said dismally. Then glancing at the tomb entrance, she told him, "Close that door and let's get away from here."

"Of course."

She stood watching as he went down the mossy stone steps and pulled the creaking iron door shut. There was a sudden rustling in the branches of the towering nearby elm tree. Involuntarily she gasped and she looked up to see a harmless gray squirrel peering down at her with open curiosity.

"What was it?" Barnabas asked, joining her again.

"A squirrel," she said, nodding to it. "I'm so on edge any sound sends a chill through me."

"No wonder," he said. "Let's move on."

They started along the path leading to the other section of the cemetery. Barnabas had his arm around her and she felt much less fear than she had before. She was anxious to get back to Collinwood and recount her experience to her father. Then he would surely help them direct a campaign to capture or kill the weird flying serpent.

She said, "Since that monster can fly it could be a great distance from here by now."

"That's the problem," Barnabas agreed.

Irma shuddered. "It was hideous!"

"I told you not to think about it!"

"It's hard to avoid that after you've seen it," she said. They were getting near the exit to the cemetery when she felt Barnabas give a start and come to a halt.

In a tense voice, he said, "Stay where you are! Don't move!

And don't look over where I'm going!"

"Why not?" Her voice was tense.

"A dead man," Barnabas said grimly. "And this one isn't buried. Wait!" And he moved away, leaving her standing there alone.

Heart thumping fiercely, she stood there and obeyed his wishes that she shouldn't look in the direction in which he'd gone. Then her nerves at the breaking point, she cried, "Barnabas!"

"All right!" he said wearily, and she heard his footsteps approaching on the hard ground. Coming up to her, he said, "The serpent has another victim."

Her eyes widened and she looked up into his solemn face. "Who?"

"Captain Westhaven," Barnabas said. "He's in the same condition as the others. Eyes staring at the sky, fear contorting his face and his throat ripped wide open."

"Oh, no!" She bent her head.

"I can't spare much sympathy on him," Barnabas said. "He had no right being here. But I can't say I like what happened to him."

"What will we do?"

"What we were planning to do," he said. "Get on back to Collinwood as quickly as we can."

"Yes," she agreed in a weak voice.

He stared at her unhappily. "You're not going to faint?"

"I'll manage."

"Sorry," he sighed. "I'll give you my arm again."

He put his arm around her once more for partial support and guidance and they left the cemetery and started the long walk up the field. As they moved on in the blazing sun she realized how dependent she had become on him. She worried that the hunt for the monster might place him in danger.

She asked him, "You weren't angry because Stuart came to the house last night?"

"No. What made you think that?"

"You left so suddenly."

"I had things to do."

"I was afraid you resented my seeing so much of him."

"I have no right to do that," he said.

"You have if you want it," she said quietly.

Barnabas offered her a sad smile. "Thanks. We'll talk about it when this is settled."

"If it ever is!"

"I think we're coming close to the end of it now."

"Don't be too sure," she worried. "I can see that the killing of the captain has already dealt us a bad blow."

"How?"

"No matter what that sailor says about him now it won't make any difference," she pointed out. "Hampstead will be acting on his own. It won't do us any good to prove that the dead man who was his partner was in the slave trade."

"You're right," Barnabas agreed. "Jim Davis has lost some of his usefulness without ever testifying."

"Now that Davis is looking after the animals on his own he isn't any too reliable." She told him about finding the sailor tormenting the lizards.

"I'm not surprised," Barnabas said. "He has a shifty air about him. But you'll have to put up with him until you can get someone better."

"I suppose so," she said. "Maybe Father will arrange to get most of the specimens sent away soon."

"It would be wise," Barnabas said.

"Hampstead gave him an ultimatum last night," she said.

They passed the old house and the stables. She saw no sign of anyone out by the stables and they moved on to Collinwood. When they entered the cool, shadowed entrance of the old mansion they were both startled to find her father talking to someone they had seen before—the supposedly bedridden Louis!

The former servant gave them a nervous glance. He still looked ill and he was unshaven, but he was dressed in passable working clothes and on his feet. Irma's father also turned to them.

Gerald Collins looked pleased. "This is Louis. He tells me he has worked here before, and I have hired him to help Jim Davis in getting some of the specimens moved from here to the railway depot."

"I see," Irma said, still in shock.

Barnabas spoke up. "We have met this man before." He turned to a sullen Louis and said, "Your health has improved very suddenly."

"I am better," Louis said in a low voice, avoiding looking at them directly. "My sickness comes and goes."

"Obviously," Barnabas said sarcastically then told Irma's father, "We have something to discuss with you in private."

"Very well," Professor Collins said, and instructed Louis, "You can go out to the stables to Jim Davis. Tell him you're to be his new helper."

"Yes, sir," the shifty Louis said and then hurried out the front door as fast as he could.

Irma turned to her father. "Do you know who he is?"

"No? Who is he?" the professor sounded surprised.

"He's the one that had the fight with the gardener. The one Mrs. Branch thinks is a little mad. They discharged him, and now you've hired him back!"

"I didn't realize!" her father protested.

"Mrs. Branch thought he might be the murderer," Barnabas explained, "and when we went down the beach to that fellow's shack he pretended to be bedridden and dying, so we put him off our suspect list."

Her father said, "He did mention that he'd been ill."

Irma gave a despairing sigh. "It doesn't matter anyhow. We know there is a feathered serpent which did the killings, so he can't possibly be guilty. But he's not a good sort to have around."

"He'll only be employed for a few days," her father said. "And what is it you have to tell me?"

Barnabas gave him a grim look. "Irma saw the flying serpent in the cemetery and Captain Westhaven was killed there by it."

"No!" the professor exclaimed.

"I'm afraid so," Barnabas said.

"Westhaven is really gone?" her father repeated.

"Yes," she said. "So there won't be any chance to use whatever Jim Davis knows about him to blacken his character."

He stared at her. "And you say you saw the creature?"

"Yes, clearly." She went on to describe where and when.

He looked shocked. "I've just about made up my mind that it does exist. That Juan found one and brought it back on his own."

Barnabas said, "There can be no doubt of that. It must be hiding in the woods or the swamp."

"The swamp would be a likely place," Gerald agreed.

"I say we should make up a group at once to find and destroy it," Barnabas said.

"That won't be easy," Mr. Collins replied.

"You can't put it off any longer, Father," Irma pointed out. "When Hampstead hears about the captain having been murdered, he'll raise a new outcry."

Barnabas nodded. "Unless you want an angry lot of protesters out here you'd better take action."

"It will be late in the day before we can start," her father said.

"We can take torches with us," Barnabas suggested. "After dark might be the best time to trap that thing."

Her father nodded. "That is true. How many will we need in the party?"

"A half-dozen or so at least," Barnabas said. "We can fan out and search an area at a time until we cover the entire woods and

swamp."
"Still it may elude us," the professor said.
"At least we'll have tried," Barnabas commented.
"Yes," the professor said reluctantly.

Irma studied him with troubled eyes. Again a shocking suspicion was forming in her mind. Once again she found herself unable to understand her father's reluctance to try to trap and destroy the monster. It made her wonder if he was really the one guilty of bringing it back from the jungle, rather than Juan. Had he merely shifted the blame to the dead man? Was he still attempting to save what he considered an invaluable specimen whether lives were lost or not?

CHAPTER 12

Irma left Barnabas and her father discussing plans for the search in the forest and the swamp beyond it. She was still troubled by her father's role in the tragedy that had overtaken Collinwood and the village, and she was by no means sure that the truth about the feathered serpent was known to them yet.

Slowly mounting the stairway, she wondered what success their attempts to catch the frightening monster would be met with. If they weren't successful, who would be the next victim? The hiring of Louis had also made her more uneasy. She was inclined to agree with Mrs. Branch that the man was mentally unstable. Having him around the estate again could add to their danger.

Irma made her way along the shadowed hallway towards her room and as she neared her door she had a fresh awareness of some menacing presence. Her hand touched the doorknob and she lingered over turning it, a tense expression on her attractive face. Something warned her that an evil threatened her on the other side of that door.

She knew that she must go on in. She had to know what it was. Slowly she turned the knob and holding her breath she eased the door open an inch at a time. Until at last the room was revealed to her and she saw that her premonition had not been fantasy.

The upper quarter pane of glass in her window had been

smashed out. Some force had swept across her dresser hurling all her personal toilet items and a lamp onto the floor. She stared with shocked eyes at the mess of wreckage on the carpet. Then she turned to her bed and saw the deep indentation on it, as if some heavy thing had come down on the center of the spread. And there on the spread was a feather, a tiny feather, of rainbow hue!

Waiting to see no more, she ran from the room and along the corridor and down the stairs. Barnabas and her father were still in the hallway and stared at her in consternation as she came rushing up to them.

"My room!" she cried. "The serpent has been there. It may still be lurking there now!"

Barnabas's face showed disbelief. "How do you know?"

"Come see for yourself," she said.

The two men went back upstairs with her and a moment later they were standing in her room surveying the damage that had been done. Barnabas went over to the bed and picked up the small feather and significantly presented it to her father.

"Incredible," Professor Collins muttered.

"The thing was in here all right," Barnabas said grimly.

"This happened since I left the house and went to the cemetery," she told them. "The serpent must have come here first and then flown to the cemetery where it attacked and killed Captain Westhaven."

Her father's eyes were troubled. "But why didn't anyone see it? Surely it would present a terrifying spectacle flying over the estate. Why didn't some of the workers see it?"

Barnabas said, "It probably has shiny scales and the feathers are so bright in color they would be lost against the light of the sun. I'd say that it would only be after sundown that it would be visible in flight."

"That's possible," the professor admitted.

"I would have thought someone would have heard the window break," Irma said.

"It's a large house," Barnabas reminded her. "You and your father were out. Most of the servants would be in the rear of the house on the lower floor, far enough away not to hear clearly."

Her eyes met his. "You can't deny the thing was here."

"We can't do that," he agreed.

"When are you leaving to look for it?"

"As soon as we can," Barnabas said. "Probably in an hour or so. It will take that long for us to organize properly."

She told them, "I'm going with you."

Her father was shocked. "That's ridiculous!"

"I appreciate your feelings," Barnabas said, smiling faintly, "but the idea of you joining the party isn't practical."

"I won't stay here!"

"Why not?" her father asked.

"It might return after you'd all gone in search of it," she said.

Barnabas said, "We'll have someone stay here and guard you."

"No," she insisted. "I want to go along. I may be able to help."

"That's unlikely," Barnabas told her. "And we may have to venture into the swamps. That's no place for a young woman."

"I'll manage," she said. "I'll get rid of these flowing skirts and wear an outfit of father's. I have done it before in the jungles."

"But there's no need now," her father protested.

"I want to go along," she said.

Barnabas gave a deep sigh. "Perhaps you are right. I'll worry less about you if you are near me. But you mustn't take any exceptional risks. You must promise to obey and do as you are told."

"I will," she promised. "I don't want to be a nuisance."

Her father was still upset at the idea. "That is what you're bound to turn out to be," he said.

"That wasn't your attitude when I accompanied you on your expeditions," she reminded him.

"It was different then," he said.

"It wasn't nearly as urgent that I be with you as it is now," she said. "I'm going and that's that."

She found suitable trousers and a jacket and had Mrs. Branch help her in dressing for the journey into the woods and swamp. The housekeeper was in a state over all that was happening.

"I declare I don't know what Collinwood is coming to," she fussed as she helped Irma into the coat jacket.

Irma surveyed herself in the mirror. She thought she looked trim and attractive. "I think the pants and coat suit me."

"But it's not fit clothing for a young lady like yourself," the older woman worried.

Irma told her, "It will be a lot better than a skirt when we reach the swamps."

"The swamp is a terrible place," Mrs. Branch warned, "full of quicksand and other evils. I don't hold with anyone going there—not to mention a young lady. After dark it's doubly dangerous."

"If we're lucky we'll catch that thing before then," Irma said.

Mrs. Branch had a dismal expression on her broad face. "I'll be locking myself in until you do return. I don't want to have any dealings with that feathered serpent."

"You're hardly safe locking yourself in," Irma warned her,

"since it did break in through my window."

"Had I known it was under this roof I'd have had a fit!" Mrs. Branch declared.

"You'll be having problems enough," Irma said. "Hampstead and the police will be arriving again to check on the murder of Captain Westhaven."

"I can't believe he's gone," the housekeeper said.

Irma's face was solemn. "There's a stable boy standing guard over his body in the cemetery at this very minute, waiting for Hampstead to arrive."

"Hampstead is a frightful man," the housekeeper said. "His face reminds me of a skull."

"I feel the same about him," Irma said. "And he is trying to make us sell the place to him."

"So many dark plots," Mrs. Branch mourned. "Who can say but he has something to do with all these murders? Just to make it appear you and your father are to blame."

Irma smiled grimly. "I appreciate your loyalty, Mrs. Branch, but we can hardly credit Hampstead with bringing back a jungle monster to harass us all. I'm afraid the blame has to be my father's or Juan's."

Mrs. Branch nodded. "Juan was a silent one. He never did become friendly with the rest of us servants."

"He didn't speak English well."

"There was more to it than that. He seemed scared all the time."

"Caring for the specimens was a nasty task."

"Those reptiles in the cellar have terrified me ever since they were brought here." Mrs. Branch sounded afraid.

"According to Father, they'll soon be sent away to different zoos."

"Maybe then I'll breathe easy again," the housekeeper said.

"I'd better go downstairs," Irma said, "or they may try to leave without me."

"That could be best."

"No," she said. "I have to do this. I want to go along." She didn't explain she had more than one reason: that the most pressing one was that she wasn't sure about her father or his sincerity in instigating the monster hunt. She feared he might still attempt to hamper their catching the horrible thing and reveal himself as the one guilty of bringing it there.

Mrs. Branch looked concerned. "Be careful in the swamp."

"I will," she said. "With luck we may not have to venture that far."

"And stay close to Mr. Barnabas," the housekeeper advised.

"I intend to," Irma said.

"He's the one best-fitted to guide you in those lonely places," she said. "He must know every inch of the ground."

Irma went downstairs expecting to see Barnabas but it was Stuart Jennings who came out of the living room to greet her in the hallway. He seemed impressed with her garb.

"You look delightful in trousers and jacket," he told her. "And I like your sweater and the cap you're wearing, but I don't approve of your going out to the swamp."

Irma looked up at him sternly. "And what do you have to say about it?"

He looked hurt. "Nothing, I suppose, though I hoped we were close enough that you'd listen to me."

Relenting a little, she gave him a small smile. "I'm sorry, Stuart. I didn't mean to bite your head off. But I do intend to go on this monster hunt, and I don't mean to let anything prevent me."

"I understand," he said. "I've heard about all the new happenings. The thing actually got into your room!"

"The evidence suggests it."

Stuart's face was grim. "That's too close for comfort. It has to be caught and killed. I've asked your father's permission to be part of the party."

"Did he give you permission?" Already she was worrying that there might be conflict between the young man and Barnabas. Barnabas had been taking charge of the organizing.

"He referred it to Barnabas and Barnabas said he'd be glad to have me come along. My special task is to stay close to you and look after your safety."

Her eyes widened. "Did he really say that?"

"He did," Stuart smiled.

"Well!" she said. Barnabas continued to offer her surprises. Apparently he was not jealous of Stuart.

They were still standing there when Barnabas came in the front door. He gave them a quick glance. "We plan to leave very shortly," he said. "One of the servants is bringing along a basket with food and drink. I doubt if we'll return until late."

Irma modeled her men's clothing for him. "I'm ready."

He gave her an indulgent smile. "I'm still against your being one of the party."

"But you will allow me to come."

Barnabas nodded. "I have no alternative. I know how stubborn you can be. You'd come after us anyway and be in even more danger. I'm assigning Jennings to keep a strict watch on you."

"So I've been told," she said.

Barnabas said, "Well, no more time for small talk. You can

join the others on the lawn."

She had wondered who would actually be included in the group and when she and Stuart went outside they discovered her father, Jim Davis, and three of the stable men. They along with Barnabas, Stuart and her would apparently comprise the search party.

Barnabas and her father led the way when they started out towards the woods. Irma kept as close to them as possible as she tried to study her father's behavior. Stuart Jennings was on one side of her and Jim Davis came limping up to join her on the other.

Giving her a knowing look with his single eye, the sailor said, "I guess this is maybe going to be the end of that feathered serpent, miss!"

"We can only hope so," she said.

Jim Davis slapped the rifle he was carrying with affection. "Let me get my sights on that critter and there won't be anything left but a lot of scattered feathers and dead snake!"

"I'd like to believe it will be that easy," she said.

Soon they reached the cemetery and began their search. In the process of this they came to the spot where one of the stable boys was guarding Captain Westhaven's ancient body. The crumpled body emphasized to all of them that this was no picnic outing. They spread across the burial ground, examining the shadows behind every gravestone, the dank interior of every vault and the branches of every shade tree.

The small group gathered outside the cemetery to hear the admission by Barnabas. "If the feathered serpent was in there it's not any longer. We'll have to try the woods."

Irma's father looked drawn and weary. "I think it's hopeless."

Barnabas frowned at him. "We're not turning back now."

The woods proved much more difficult than the cemetery. The ground was uneven; the forest was almost impenetrable at places; and there was constant harassment by huge flies with painful stings.

Irma and Stuart had become isolated from the others. As they went on through areas of dense thickets their progress became much slower. Irma was weary, and a glance at the perspiring, grimy face of the man at her side told her that he must be just as tired.

"We don't want to get too far from the others," he worried.

"We're to meet at the edge of the swamp, aren't we?"

Stuart halted and took a deep breath and nodded. "Yes. We better be there before dark or we could get lost in these woods."

"They don't go back that far, do they?" she asked. She hadn't thought of this possibility before.

"They merge with the swamp at one point," he told her. "We

don't want to get in there. It's bad ground to face alone."

"It doesn't seem as if we're going to find that awful thing," she said. "They were supposed to fire a shot if they came on anything."

"I wish they'd fire one anyway," he worried. "It would give us a hint of where they are."

She halted and looked up at him worriedly. "Don't you know?"

"I have an idea," he said noncommittally.

They struggled on through the thick brush and saw no sign of the reptilian creature they sought. Then from the right and a distance ahead there came the sound of a shot, followed shortly after by another. They exchanged excited glances and Stuart began heading in the direction from which the sound had come.

Irma kept up with him slightly out of breath as she stumbled over the uneven ground and pushed between the bushes. "Do you think they've found it?"

"There were two shots," he told her. "It sounds promising."

"I hope so," she said grimly. "I hope we manage to destroy it after all this."

Stuart waited for her and then gave her his arm for support. "You wanted to come," he reminded her.

"I had to," she said, without attempting to explain why.

In about five minutes they emerged into a clearing and found the others. The minute she saw their relaxed attitude and noted they were having their dinner she knew the gunshots had been a signal and not directed at the feathered serpent.

Barnabas came forward to greet them and confirmed this. He said, "I fired the shots because you hadn't gotten here. I was afraid you might be lost."

"I'd say we were," Stuart confessed.

Irma gave Barnabas a worried look. "No sign of anything?"

"Not yet," he said. "As soon as we rest a little and finish eating we'll light our torches and move on into the swamps. I don't think you and Jennings should venture beyond this point. You can wait here for us."

"No," she protested. "We want to do our share."

"Naturally," Stuart agreed.

"It's going to be very dangerous," Barnabas warned. "There are quicksands, deep, treacherous pools, almost impenetrable areas of thick brush."

"We've managed this far," she said. "And with the torches it will be easier to keep in contact with the others." That ended the discussion. She saw that Barnabas was standing up to the strain of the search better than her father and most of the others. Jim Davis, who had a bad limp in any case, was walking now as if each step was painful to him.

As they began their assault of the swamp with burning torches in hand the sailor came over to her for a moment and said, "I hope this gets finished pretty quick, miss. My leg is giving out on me."

"Why don't you tell Barnabas and wait here?" she asked.

He shook his head. "I'm not one to give up, miss," he rasped wearily.

Irma and Stuart were assigned to a path where the ground was better, but even there the swamp was menacing. With darkness at hand fog raised over the murky pools to make the place a misty, jungle nightmare. She walked at the young man's side, glancing fearfully around her, feeling she was back in those feared Mexican jungles. The torch reflected on young Jenning's grimy face, giving him a look of desperation. "We'll never find anything here," he told her as they pushed further into the foggy maze of weirdly shaped trees and dank pools.

Suddenly she heard the flutter of wings just above her and stumbled back, almost dropping her torch. Her cry of fear rang out in the night and she grasped out for Stuart.

He was at once beside her. "Don't worry," he consoled her. "It was only an owl."

"Oh, no!" She closed her eyes a moment, her heart pounding crazily.

"Want to go back?" he asked.

"Not yet," she said firmly, and to prove her determination she forced herself on ahead of him.

She didn't want to give in to the terror that had grown more intense since they'd entered the swamp. She didn't want Stuart to guess how near the breaking point she was. Suddenly she heard a strange, gasping cry from behind her and at once wheeled around to see that Stuart had fallen face forward on the rough ground and his torch had fallen into a great puddle of water near him and been extinguished.

"Stuart!" she cried and knelt by him, not knowing what had happened.

Then she heard the other sound—the weird hissing sound of a serpent. She looked up to see the feathered serpent above her, ready to descend on her. She gave a wild scream and scrambled back over the soggy ground, holding her torch high.

At the same time she became vaguely aware of something else... of a figure standing behind the monstrous feathered serpent. Then she saw that the serpent was in reality a fake, stuffed thing held forward by the man with a pole.

The man was Jim Davis.

Davis gave a rasping laugh and tossed the dummy reptile aside. At the same time he took a knife from his belt. "You didn't expect it to be me, did you?" he asked. But his voice no longer had that weird rasp and it sounded familiar.

She continued to back away, holding out the flaming torch as a weapon. "Who are you?" she demanded.

His answer was to rip off the eye patch, and as he advanced on her, he sneered and said, "You didn't think I'd let you and your father get away with cheating me, did you?"

She recognized him. "Quentin!" she gasped. "Quentin Collins! You're the one!"

He nodded, leering at her. "I created the dummy serpent and did the killings. I hid it out here to wait for my chance to get you. Your father will be next, or maybe Barnabas. Then there'll be no one to stand between me and Collinwood!"

He made a wild lunge for her and she thrust the torch in his face. With a snarl of rage he brushed it aside and ripped it from her hand. But by this time Stuart had recovered consciousness and was on his feet. He attacked Quentin just in time to save Irma from the knife. She stood by in the darkness as the two men struggled and rolled about on the marshy ground at her feet. There was nothing she could do. She had no idea where Stuart's gun had fallen.

She screamed repeatedly and then saw the reflection of distant torches in the mist. A moment later a group headed by Barnabas reached the scene in time to help Stuart subdue the apparently insane Quentin. As soon as the black sheep of the Collins family knew that struggle was useless he gave in. Barnabas attempted to question him but he relapsed into a sullen silence.

Barnabas came over to her. "Are you hurt?"

"No," she said, and still breathless, told him what happened.

Barnabas found the dummy feathered serpent in a pool of water and recovered it to show it to Professor Collins. "There is your monster," he said. "Not very frightening without the evil of Quentin behind it."

Professor Collins stared at it sadly. "I knew there was no such creature. The Aztecs created it out of their imaginations. I always felt that."

Stuart turned to her. "I let you down at the worst possible time," he said. "They shouldn't have trusted you in my care."

"It wasn't your fault," she told him. "You weren't expecting Quentin to come and attack you from the rear."

"I should have been more on the alert," he said unhappily, and for the rest of the trip back he avoided her, walking ahead with the stable men.

Barnabas had tied Quentin's hands behind his back and was leading his silent prisoner towards Collinwood. Irma walked with her father. They had almost reached the edge of the woods when suddenly a strange, blood-curdling howl rang from Quentin's lips. In the next instant a huge greenish-yellow wolf stood where he had been. It gave a great leap and vanished into the woods. Barnabas raised his rifle and blazed a shot after the creature, as did one of the stable men. But neither of the shots found their mark. They could hear the renegade animal go on crashing through the woods a distance away.

Barnabas turned to the others. "It's no use," he said. "We'd never catch him."

"Will he return?" her father wanted to know.

"Not for a long while," Barnabas said grimly. "You can be sure of that. And never as Jim Davis. So you'll not be tormented by a feathered serpent any longer."

"Will Saul Hampstead believe the explanation?" Gerald Collins worried.

Barnabas smiled grimly. "He doesn't have much choice."

This proved true. Hampstead raged about his friend being murdered and still tried to make it seem that the Collinses were to blame. But there were no more murders or terrifying appearances of the weird feathered serpent, so the villagers were content with the explanation it had been killed in the swamp.

Within a short time Professor Collins sent all the live specimens on to zoos in Boston and New York. Collinwood was restored to a placid, country mansion. True, Irma was still conscious of the brooding presence of phantoms of other tragic days. But these long-ago ghosts did nothing to harm her as the malicious Quentin had. She had no idea where he had escaped to, and one evening some weeks later as she strolled in the moonlight with Barnabas, she asked his opinion. He was loath to give any exact answer.

"I wouldn't want to guess where he has gone," Barnabas said. "But you can be sure he is alive and well somewhere."

"What makes him so evil?" she wondered.

A thoughtful expression crossed his handsome face. "I don't think he wants to be evil. It is the curse. He's unable to fight it. That has been his tragedy. And he does love Collinwood or he wouldn't keep returning here in one guise or another."

"And you?"

The moonlight made it easy to see his smile. "Of course I also love Collinwood," he said.

"Now that you have been cured of your strange illness, there is no reason why you shouldn't remain here," she said. "Father is leaving on another expedition shortly. It will be very lonely here for me."

Barnabas studied her with gentle eyes. "I wish I could stay with you. I wish that I knew I was cured permanently, but I daren't risk asking you to be the wife of a man who might at any time lapse into a nightmare."

"I'm willing to take that risk," she said.

"Give me time to think about it," he begged her. He took her in his arms for a lasting kiss before they walked back to Collinwood.

No more was said of the future but Irma continued to hope that he would see things her way.

But one morning the old house was empty again and a brief note was left with one of the stable hands for her. Barnabas begged her forgiveness and warned her there was no point in her waiting for him.

So the romance ended as quickly as it had begun.

Stuart Jennings somehow heard that her father was soon leaving for Africa. He came to see her one afternoon in early October. It had been several months since they'd met. For a little while there was an awkwardness between them but it passed.

They walked to Widows' Hill and there he turned to her and said, "I know you were in love with Barnabas."

"Well?" she said.

His eyes met hers. "I also know that it could never work out, that Barnabas has gone. I've no pride where you're concerned. I don't think pride is nearly as important as love. So I'm asking to be your second choice."

She looked up into his pleading, boyish face and was touched by his frankness. Softly she said, "I've always liked you. You know that."

"Will you be my wife?"

She nodded. "If you like. I can't promise undying love from this moment. But I believe I will come to love you in time."

Stuart smiled. "We'll be very happy." He took her in his arms, but even as their lips met Irma had a momentary vision of the sad-faced man in the caped-coat—the man she would never entirely forget.